HANDSOME DEVIL

Quantrin Nights #1

Written by

Gael Romer

HANDSOME DEVIL

Cover art by Nyco Rudolph
Cover typeface by Fontdation

ISBN: 978-1-0688780-1-5 (hc)
ISBN: 978-1-0688780-0-8 (pbk)
ISBN: 978-1-0688780-2-2 (ebook)

First edition paperback July 2024
2345678910

Rocket Dame Publishing Ltd.
rocketdame.com

For G, without whom I may never have had the audacity.

1

Haez

Haez was supposed to be celebrating. Alone, sure, but today was when he finally expected to pay off his debts and he wanted his first night of true freedom to be spent with a stein of cheap brew. Instead, he found his head being knocked sideways by another punch, this one sending a loose incisor rattling across the synthsteel floor.

He groaned and lifted his head back to centre, twisting his hands against his binds to relieve some of the pressure. The rough chair of repurposed metal mesh was rubbing sores into his burgundy skin, even through his clothing. Squinting through the blood dripping down over his eye, he looked back at his captor.

The thin, pale human man known only as Mr. Staukar sat in a much finer throne, made of twisted wrought ebion that wound itself into elegant vines from the legs to the high back. This tower level wasn't much more than a converted warehouse, but it suited Staukar's purposes—plus, it saved him the energy of getting blood out of carpeting. Throughout the room were a few dozen members of the Sabres, lazily slinging their guns and chuckling at the expense of the sad sacks getting worked over by the boss' second, Vrix. The massive, four-armed yreet stepped to the side after striking Haez, wiping the blood from his knuckles and looking to his boss.

Staukar looked impassively to the three captives: an emaciated yreet, a bloody-but-proud human, and Haez. His crescent horns were flaky with his own blood and the deep hollows of his face had collected bile from the last time Vrix slammed one of those huge fists into his stomach. The unlucky trio of men who'd had the misfortune of pissing off Staukar. The mobster leaned his elbow into the arm of the chair and rested his chin on his fist, looking like a king surveying his favourite jester. All he offered them was an amused smile before speaking again.

"That's the second time you've mentioned level-checks, Haez. It doesn't answer the question of where my shipment is. I know you wouldn't have let the cops take it. After all, that would have been a very stupid thing for a smart mephite like you to do."

Haez spit the blood bubbles from his lips and replied, "One of the security guards recognized me. I didn't have a choice. I have outstanding warrants and he would've turned me in."

"So instead of pissing off the local authorities, you chose to piss on my hospitality? I gave you this job to clear out the debt you already owe me, Haez. Because I like you. And this is what I get?" Staukar winced theatrically and pressed a hand over his heart.

The human man to Haez's left scoffed, spat at Staukar's display, and said, "I've paid you back what I owe you three times over. I'm not letting you milk me for money anymo—"

He didn't finish his sentence before Staukar snapped his fingers and pointed at him. One of the thugs behind him raised his gun and fired a single neat laser-bolt between his eyes. The man's head jolted back and stilled. Staukar almost seemed bored as he turned to the remaining two.

"That's a shame. Money owed will have to be redistributed," he sighed, looking expectantly at the two remaining captives. The wheels in Haez's head turned quickly: Staukar already knew that none of them had the money they owed him, so this couldn't be a shakedown, and he couldn't get what he was owed if it was a group execution—why bring them all together if it was just to kill them? Unless he wanted to thin the herd of losers in his service and send a message at the same time.

No, it wasn't a shakedown. It was a competition.

Without thinking, Haez blurted, "I have a job lined up. Real big take, enough to pay back everyone's debt."

Staukar turned his attention back to Haez, eyes glittering with interest. "And what is this big job?"

"I have a friend—"

"No, you don't," laughed Staukar, leaning forward like a cat watching prey. Haez clenched his jaw and focused on the pain in his empty tooth socket to keep down his rising panic.

"I have a friend," he continued carefully. "They got it all set up for me. I was going to meet them to go over details when Vrix picked me up. I swear on my father's grave."

The thin yreet to his right caught on to what was happening too late. Looking from Haez to Staukar, he started, "M-me too. A good job. Better t-than his."

Staukar flicked the yreet a disdainful glance and snapped his fingers again. Another laser bolt tore through the air and the yreet was silenced. Haez didn't look, trying to focus on Staukar.

Hells, I think I knew that guy.

Staukar's face split into a cold grin. "I guess my favourite mephite gets another chance." He gave a nod to Vrix, who returned to Haez and started releasing his binds. As he was untied, Staukar reached into his breast pocket and produced a little pad of flex.

While he scribbled onto one of the pages, he said, "You have two days, Haez. That's your outstanding debts, the debts of these two, interest, and emotional damages."

Haez stood gingerly from his seat, rubbing at his wrists and trying to not flex his bruised abdomen. He hobbled towards Staukar to take the sheet while Vrix wrapped the ropes neatly between his hand and his elbow.

Plucking it from Staukar's hand, he asked, "Emotional damages? Really?"

Staukar gave him another cold sneer, "I'm sensitive. Two days."

· · · · ● · ● · · · ·

A rolling side door banged up and Haez was thrown headfirst out of the tower and into the metal railing that ringed the exterior walkway, cracking off part of one of his horns and sending it clanging and banging off the lower walkways. He lay there in a crumpled heap as his coat and weather-beaten satchel were thrown unceremoniously on top of him. The door slammed down and somewhere far below, Haez heard the distant yelp of someone being hit by his horn.

The city planet of Quantrin sprawled out above and below him, each of the kilometres-high skyscrapers projecting walkways like spokes on infinite stacked wheels. The spokes connected towers, merged into open platforms, and split apart again to make room for cramped glider lanes. The latticework of rickety synthsteel repeated every hundred metres going up the towers, dividing the city into layers of strata with the wealthiest perched at the top, held close to the sun by the impoverished below.

Haez stayed there a long while, his body too bruised to do anything but melt into the grating underfoot. When he finally did shamble up, he clung to the loose railing to drag himself to his feet. He rubbed at the aching base of his broken horn, but looking over the edge of the walkway, he knew he was lucky that his horn was all that dropped into the abyss.

He flinched as he slung on his coat and satchel and shuffled to check his reflection in a panel of flexiglass. He grimaced at what he saw: the broken horn might have been ruggedly handsome, but the image was ruined by the missing tooth, blackened eye, and fist-shaped bruises turning his red face a muddy purple. He dug in his satchel for a bottle of water to rinse the lingering blood out of his mouth, as well as splash it on his face. He had to scrub his fingers into his deep cheek hollows and around his horn bases to get rid of the lingering filth.

When he was satisfied with the results, he hobbled as naturally as possible to leave the narrow maintenance lane and join the bustling foot traffic on the wide spoke of the main concourse, having to hunch in on himself to squeeze between pedestrians. The mesh metal canopy shielding the walkway at least cast some shadow over his face. He listened to the constant plinking sound of both rain and garbage bouncing off the roof overhead while he got lost in his thoughts.

Two days. That's all he had to turn his desperate lie into a reality. And now, on top of his already-insurmountable debts, he was saddled with the debts of his less-fortunate fellows. *At least you're not dead,* he reminded himself. He definitely knew that yreet. His stomach twisted at the realisation that he couldn't remember his name at all. No one would find out what happened to him for months.

Focus. He needed a lead and there was only one person he knew he could always trust. *Ottok,* he thought. *Good old Ottok never lets me down.* He considered calling his wristcom but rejected the idea. This was a big ask and it needed a personal touch. With purpose in his step, he set out towards Ottok's unit, praying his old friend would be able to pull through for him again.

. . . . ● . ● . ● . . ●

"Ottok! Ottok, pal, you home?" Haez banged his fist against the sliding door of Ottok's unit. The old gallan hardly ever left his workshop, but it would just be Haez's luck to get there while he was out on a liquor run. He paused and listened at the door. There was definitely rustling inside. He banged his fist again and yelled, "I can hear you, Ottok! This is important!"

The intercom above the door gave a staticky crackle but no voice came out. Haez shifted uncomfortably, glancing up at the speaker.

"You there?" He asked upwards.

A buzzing sigh came out followed by Ottok's voice, asking, "What do you want?" Haez's mind went into overdrive. Was Ottok pissed off at him too? What had he done to Ottok?

"Listen, Ottok, I'll be honest with you—"

He was cut off by a rueful bark of laughter from the crackling speaker. "I'd pay good money to see you being honest. You coming to ask for more money to waste betting on rixies? You never paid me back for the last loan." Haez squeezed his eyes shut and pounded the heel of his palm against his forehead. *Hells, the fucking rixie loan,* he thought. He cleared his throat and tried to continue without letting the distress into his voice.

"Yeah, I-I'm working on it. That's why I'm here. I'm just trying to get a job to get back the last of what I owe you. Do you know about any good leads? Smuggling, bounties, empty vacation homes? I'm open to anything right now."

The aging video monitor at the top corner of the door frame struggled to flicker to life, its juddering display showing Ottok's dour, avian face—his beak covered with studs and hoops through drilled holes. He glowered down and Haez squirmed under his scrutiny, unused to Ottok looking at him with such disdain.

Finally, Ottok twitched his head to the side and said, "I might have something. Someone looking for an extraction."

Haez's shoulders sagged with relief and he scrambled to get his datapad out of his satchel, ready to note down all the details. "You're my hero, Ottok. What's the target?"

"Target is your head. Has to be extracted from your ass. Don't come here again."

With that, the video feed and speaker both went dead. Haez stood dumbstruck for a moment before tentatively knocking at the door again. "Ottok?"

No reply. He pulled back to start pounding the door again, but stopped himself at the last second. Instead, he leaned forward and pressed his remaining horn against the wall wearily. If even Ottok wouldn't help him . . .

He took a deep breath and pulled himself up from the wall. This was no time to be feeling sorry for himself. Turning to leave Ottok's unit, he tapped into his wristcom and brought up the list of his contacts. Personal touches be damned—the only way he was going to find anyone still willing to throw him a bone was by testing as many burnt bridges as possible.

· · · ● · ● · ● · ● · ● · ● · ·

It took hours of scrubbing through his contacts before he found someone still willing to work with him. It seemed like every person was another that he owed money or a favor or a job. Those didn't get under his skin nearly as much as the ones that just plain didn't like him.

When he finally did get a bite, it wasn't his first choice: The Delnul Brothers. They were a pair of twins that used to be more active as freelancers until they fell in with the Sabres six cycles ago. It wouldn't do for Staukar to find out that Haez had lied to his face, but he was hardly in any position to be picky.

Still, he didn't relish having to work with them. Proll could be good company if you ever got him away from his brother, but Rakir gave Haez the creeps. He was a fixer for Staukar, and you could see from the flat deadness in his eyes that the 'one-too-many' murder threshold had long-since been overstepped.

They agreed to meet him at his favourite bar, *Chenian's Rest.* Not a favourite for the ambiance or menu, but it was popular among freelancers as a public space for contract negotiations. The stink of stale brew and body odour was enough to keep the polite company out and anyone willing to endure the stench knew to mind their own business.

The door slid open to let him into the soup and he scanned over the patrons for the thick horns and pallid blue skin of the twins. At a back table, one set of horns jutted into the air. He sidestepped between the cramped mesh tables to reach his contact, silently willing it would be mildly pleasant Proll and not unsettling Rakir.

It was Rakir. *Shit.* He gave his most winning smile, even as he couldn't stop nervously tonguing the empty socket where his tooth used to be.

Rakir stiffened and drew back slightly at Haez's appearance like some of the sweat and grime might leap across the table to sully his own pristine clothes. With a disgust-laced stare, he gave an abrupt, "Sit."

"Don't mind if I do. Uh, how have you been? Proll around?"

Rakir ignored the question and said in that same affectless manner, "Two thousand for the info." Haez quickly tossed a loaded credit chit across the table to him.

Rakir touched his wristcom to the chit and when it gave a cheerful beep, he reached into his coat for a folio of flex. He flopped it on the table in front of Haez, who snatched it up and read greedily.

His face fell, and as he went on to each subsequent page, his stomach dropped more and more. Rakir snapped open a nicostick and started sucking in the fumes while Haez considered the trash he just emptied his accounts for.

"Some rich old lady. Out of town for the weekend. Lots of good stuff. Collectors will pay for it."

"I can see that. How exactly am I supposed to get in?"

"Blueprints and security systems are in there." Haez could feel his blood pressure rising at the flippant reply.

"I can see that too. I can see that I would need to spend twice what I just paid you to get half of what I need to crack this security. I want my money back," He bit out.

Rakir just shrugged, "Sorry, you saw the job. No refunds now. You needed something big, right?"

"Something big?! Rakir, this—" He stopped himself and lowered his voice before the other patrons started staring, "There's a reason why no one picks up jobs like this—they're impossible. Suicidal even."

Rakir thought about this and gave Haez a cold stare. "Hm. Well, give Staukar my regards."

He was right, of course. Haez looked back to his folio and muttered, "At least give me back enough to get some security spikes."

Rakir shook his head, "You wanted a job. You got a job. The rest is your problem."

Haez wiped a hand down his face and covered his mouth, stuck in thought. If he could pull it off, he'd have enough to pay off Staukar, plus all his other debts. He might even have enough left over to get off this hellhole. Maybe go back home.

He just needed to decide how to fund the venture. He still had his gun, but the thought of armed robbery made his skin crawl.

The door to the bar swished open. Haez glanced towards the sound and did a double take. Finally, the universe was on his side. Wandering in with a face as bright and innocent as sunshine was a human girl, glancing wide-eyed at her surroundings and tucking her long, wavy hair behind her ear like a nervous tic. Shy, frail, and practically shivering with excitement or fear inside a coat that looked big enough to fit Haez.

It was probably the first thing she was able to buy outside the spaceport. Probably the first time away from her home world. Probably scared and just needing a friend to show her the ropes.

Easy money.

Haez tried to straighten himself out, smoothing out his collar and giving his horns a quick wipe with a napkin.

"May I?" he asked, grabbing Rakir's brew stein without waiting for an answer. He held it up to examine his reflection, rubbing the lingering rusty flakes from around his copper eyes and practicing his smile—one that obscured his missing tooth.

"How do I look?"

"Like day-old shit." Rakir snatched back his glass and followed Haez's gaze. "A human? Really?"

Haez clammed up at the question. "They're not that bad. Besides, you're the one who wouldn't give me any money back."

Rakir gave his head a disdainful shake before turning back to his drink. Haez shoved the folio into the inside pocket of his coat and left Rakir to his drinking.

The girl had found her way to the bar and was showing her inexperience through every action. Scattered across the counter were little plasteen drink menus, added to accommodate more tourist traffic. The play didn't work, and the menus sat untouched, growing a thick coat of grease and fuzz—until now, where this naïve little human had one of the grungy things held an inch from her nose. Haez peered over her shoulder to see what was tripping her up as she muttered.

"G . . . guth . . . guthil?" she mumbled, pushing her honey-brown hair away from her face and squinting down at the card.

"Close, it's *thughil*," he said close to her ear. She jumped and whipped around to face him, and his heart fluttered. She was pretty in a human way; big, brown eyes, pillowy lips and pink cheeks on a face that only reached as high as his chest. Haez's mind nearly went blank thinking about how nice she smelled. She gave a nervous little laugh and looked down at the menu, still clutched in her little hands.

"That's embarrassing. I know how to read, just . . . not this. I shouldn't just rely on . . . " she trailed off, tapping the spot behind her ear where everyone had their translator chips implanted.

"You must be new to the planet. Yreet is the standard in these parts." Haez immediately felt like kicking himself. The girl deflated at his words as the scraps of confidence left her body.

"I should have waited at the spaceport. God, I should go, I—"

"Wait, I'm sorry." Haez shifted to block her exit ever-so-slightly. "It's nothing to be embarrassed about. We all start somewhere. You, uh, probably shouldn't start with *thughil,* though. It's strong enough to burn a hole in *my* stomach. May I?" He gestured at the menu. She handed it over sheepishly and sat down onto a stool, twisting her hands together.

He scanned the list of overpriced mixed drinks and cast a sideways look at his target. Definitely a sweet drink person. He flagged over the bartender and ordered a brew for himself and a double Ozarlan Sunrise for the girl—some fruity mess with enough clashing sweeteners and colourants to churn Haez's stomach.

"Which one did you order?" she asked. Haez just gave her a wink with his practiced smile.

"Trust me," he replied, passing her the drink. She took a cautious little sip and her face lit up before taking a heavy gulp. The brightening of her eyes and bobbing of her throat made Haez's pants tighten.

He cleared his throat and ploughed on. "So, uh, y-you mentioned the spaceport?"

She hummed in agreement mid-sip. "Yeah, my transport has a layover for a few hours. I thought I would come here to pass some time. You can probably tell I've not been away from home much and, well . . . " Her tone turned furtive and her eyes grew a little wild when she continued, "My parents would never let me come somewhere like this."

"Your parents? You sure you're old enough to be in here?" She snorted into her drink and shoved his shoulder. Harder than expected—the drink must've gone to her head already.

"Shut up, it's not a crime to listen to your parents. Still, I'm going to Weizzi for the university and being away from them is going to be niiiiiiice." She drew out the last syllable, making herself giggle.

"Not going to the dorms, are you?" The thought of her surrounded by parties and drunk college boys made Haez bristle for reasons he couldn't explain. He untensed when she shook her head emphatically.

"Not me. Not a party person. I don't get invited and I wouldn't want to go anyways."

"Pretty lady like you? I bet you'd have men tripping over each other to talk to you."

The smile she gave him was a little sad. "Now you're just trying to flatter me."

"Is it working?"

She reached up to pluck off a bit of napkin that had snagged on his broken horn, and relaxed back down, resting her cheek in her hand. "You know, you're not so bad yourself."

• • • ● • ● • • •

Minutes slid into hours of easy conversation, and without realizing, Haez was drinking up every detail she offered like they were gifts. She was majoring in economics but would rather be doing culinary studies. She was reading a romance book right now and was too embarrassed to tell him the plot. She loved plants. Haez couldn't remember the last time it had been this easy to talk to *anyone*, let alone a pretty human who smelled sweeter than a song.

Every easy smile and laugh she granted him just made what he had to do worse. *It's easy money,* he kept reminding himself. *This or your neck.*

"And then," she giggle-snorted in the middle of her story, "we climb on the roof and—" she broke down again and couldn't even finish her own sentence without wheezing. Haez wrapped a hand around her waist and pulled her in. The coat at least had roomy pockets. He slipped his hand in and delicately felt around for something the right shape and size for a chit case. The girl was oblivious, nuzzling into his collar like an overly affectionate cat. He bumped into a moulded shape, which he palmed and slid up his sleeve.

"I'm starting to think you've had too much to drink, pretty lady," he laughed, trying to pull back. She wrapped her arms around his midsection, trapping him in place.

"Nooooo, I'm fine," she slurred. "We should get another round."

"You sure? What time was your transport leaving?"

She froze and jerked upright, swaying on her stool. "Oh no. Oh, god, how long has it been?"

"A couple hours, I think. Is everything okay?"

She jumped off her stool and nearly fell backwards into a neighboring table. He grabbed her elbow to steady her, letting the touch linger longer than needed.

"If I miss it, my parents are going to kill me. I'm so sorry, I just—" she gestured back towards the door. Haez nodded and gave her a little wave.

"You take care, pretty lady. Maybe I'll see you around some time."

She gave him one last smile. "Yeah. I think I'd like that, Haez."

And with that, she vanished out the door. Haez sat silently in her wake for a moment before sliding the chit case back into his hand.

He hated himself. He wished he could call back every person he contacted earlier to let them know that he got it now—he wouldn't want to work with him, either. He popped the case, hoping that it would at least have enough to make his conscience go silent. It opened to show—

Nothing.

Not a single chit. No ID. Just a single piece of folded flex. He opened the flex and read one word.

Sucker

His heart stopped in his chest. "What the fuck?" he muttered, staring at the paper. Suddenly the gears in his head clicked together.

They'd never exchanged names.

He patted down his coat to find it also empty, the flex folio gone. His one ticket out of this mess and it had vanished along with the nameless girl.

Haez bolted for the door, jamming himself through the gap before it could even fully slide open. He scanned the walkways and platforms for glossy waves of human hair on that perfect human head with a wringable human neck.

Gone. Impossibly gone already. And with her went the last of Haez's credits and his last chance to save his own skin. All he could do was scream uselessly into the echoing skyscrapers.

"FUCK YOU, PRETTY LADY!"

2

Sonia

Sonia knew that she only had twenty seconds to get out of dodge before the sucker from the bar caught on. As soon as she heard the door slide shut behind her, she dropped the drunken stumble and straightened into a power walk towards her planned escape route. Not too fast—a running human might draw attention, and she needed to vanish.

The stupid wig was the first thing to go. She pulled it off and tossed it over a railing to vanish into the lower levels. Next was the oversized coat. Ottok knew the loser had a thing for delicate little humans, and there were only so many ways to hide her thickly muscled torso. *Good riddance,* she thought, rolling her shoulders and scratching at her scruffy hair, blissfully free from the cheap wig.

She slipped down a narrow service path and at the end was a fire escape ladder that she'd stuffed a pack behind. She pulled it out and shoved the folio inside before climbing to a vantage point. The smart thing to do would be to get as far away as possible.

But Ottok really didn't like this guy, and she had a feeling he'd put on a good show.

He didn't disappoint. Moments after she took a seat on the rooftop, Haez burst out of the bar looking ready to kill. She had to fight back a laugh—she didn't know he would get that red and angry. It would have been kind of hot if it weren't so pathetic.

After looking every way but up, he screamed out into the night and stormed away from the bar.

"Sorry, babe," she murmured at his retreating back. It startled her how much she meant it. She had pulled this scam a hundred times before, but usually the targets were stinking lugs. If their hands weren't trying to grope her, they were trying to jack themselves off under the table without her noticing. Not Haez, though. He'd smiled at her. Made her laugh. Treated her like a person.

It helped that unlike most of the low-lives she targeted, there was something about him that really did it for her. Her grandmother had always referred to mephites as 'those Devil-men,' and he certainly looked the part, with his rich, rusty skin, sharply angular features, and imposingly tall frame. And even with the busted horn, missing tooth and swollen eye, there was the way he looked at her like she was the shining centre of the galaxy—and the smile that said he loved being in her gravitational pull. If she didn't know about his history of fucking up contracts and blowing money that wasn't his, she'd have almost thought he was . . . sweet.

She gave her head a shake. He wasn't. They were both playing characters and his just happened to make her heart flutter a bit. "Get it together, Sonia," she said quietly to herself. "You're too old for that teenager bullshit."

To get her mind back on business, she pulled out the folio to see what'd gotten Haez so worked-up. She was soaking in the details when her wristcom beeped—Ottok checking in on her. She clicked him through without looking up. A holographic projection of the rotund gallan appeared in front of her.

"Hi, Dad," she said, giving him a toothy grin.

The chicken man gave a disgruntled sigh and clicked his beak in annoyance. "Don't call me that. You find Haez?"

She nodded. "Mmm hmm, right where you said he'd be. I don't think he likes me much."

Ottok gave a bark of laughter. "Predictable bastard. Did he actually find someone who would give him a lead?"

"My lead now. He got it from some big, blue mephite guy. Do you know if he's legit? This job is . . . yikes."

"Sounds like one of the Delnul boys," he replied, his face turning concerned. "You might want to drop that one."

"Really? It'll be tough to pull off, but there's a lot of money here. Hey, if I can borrow some of your stuff, we can split it! Fifty-fifty on whatever you're able to get for it all," she said, getting excited.

"Sonia, I don't think—"

"Come on, if I can pull this off, I'll be the best goddamn cat burglar on Quantrin! Let me try at least."

Ottok was quiet and thoughtful for a moment. "You really need to work on your haggling. Fifty-fifty is a lousy deal for you if you're doing all the work."

She deflated at that. She knew he was looking out for her, but it stung to be reminded that even after eight years on the planet, she still needed Ottok to tell her what she should be paid. Something in her brain just never clicked onto how to do it. Lockpicking and scamming were easy. Putting aside her sentimentality long enough to argue a fair wage? That was hard.

"Should I have done sixty-forty?"

"Should have started at eighty-twenty and let me argue you up. Too late now—you rang the bell. Fifty-fifty it is."

"Gee, thanks, Dad. Load me up in the morning?"

"Fine, but stop calling me that."

She raised a hand to wave him off and he disconnected, his holo-gram fizzling out. She took one last look out over the city in the direction that Haez went.

It was a shame. He really *was* sweet.

3

Haez

Haez was a strong believer in the healing powers of a good night's sleep, even though he rarely got them anymore.

Even as he was simmering with stale rage, he made a point to sleep in and go through his morning routine of tending to his plants. The pretty con-artist wouldn't be able to make any moves until the evening and he needed his mind clear if he was going to catch the bitch.

Haez's otherwise-bare unit was covered in greenery. It reminded him of his home planet and its treetop cities. Quantrin had no green, except what the wealthy could import and the botanically-minded could sprout from stolen clippings. It was risky, but on the occasions where his deliveries took him to upper level parties, he would always try to smuggle away some small plant by tucking it inside his coat like a treasure. There would be trouble if he was caught in some aristocrat's garden with pocket shears, but it was worth it. Everything else he owned that could be sold had long since been traded away. But never the plants.

As he went through watering, pruning, and checking the leaves for rot, he thought about the girl. Humans weren't uncommon on Quantrin, but human women experienced enough to get one over on Haez? Those were rare. There was no way she had gotten as good as she was without racking up a record as extensive as his. And police records were open to the public.

With a clear mind, he set aside the watering can and moved to his terminal to start the search. Just because police records were public didn't mean they were accessible. Instead of a tidy database of offenders, he found himself having to scrub through the daily listings of bookings, and anyone as good as her wouldn't have been caught that often. He scanned through them until his eyes felt glazed-over and droopy. When she finally did appear, he nearly passed her by, but the sly grin shining out of the screen knocked the tiredness back out of him.

The woman staring out of the mugshot was nothing like the nervous, wide-eyed girl he had pegged as easy money. Her hair was chopped short and shaggy, probably done herself with no help but a mirror. In retrospect, the near-black was a much more natural fit for her tawny complexion than the light-brown wig. The coat was definitely a conscious choice too. Her whole body was densely corded with muscle. She'd probably had to rip half the filling out of the thing so it would hang off her like it was being held up by narrow, bony shoulders.

Judging from the smug, ruthless face of Sonia Jentis, he wasn't the first sucker she had pulled this bit on. He'd never stood a chance.

Sonia. He rolled the name around his mouth. *God damn, what a woman.*

He froze with that thought and gave his head a shake. He couldn't be thinking that. He wouldn't allow it. He pushed it away and tried to refocus on feeling nothing but bright, clean anger. *I bet she doesn't even like plants, the bitch,* he thought.

Once he had found her, her long and winding record was open. He was damned lucky to have found her at all. The charge that brought her up was from months ago when she was caught trying to breach a window. After that, it had been years since the last time she'd been picked up—definitely better than his track record. And the lost little human scam must have been working well for her. There was no sign that cops had even gotten a sniff of it. The small smattering of arrests were all attempted burglaries, which gave him a strange sense of satisfaction. Even if he couldn't find her, at least she would be able to make use of what she stole off him.

Hells, maybe she would get too cocky and get locked up again. A guy could dream.

He moved past these to the useful bits—her earliest crimes and by far the densest part of her record. Petty theft, pickpocketing, vandalism, a healthy mix for an aspiring criminal who had yet to hone her skills—and all in the same neighbourhood, like any amateur. She might as well have painted a target on her home turf.

None of this told him an address, though. Haez went back to his wristcom and mulled over the last handful of contacts he hadn't tried the night before. Even if one of them knew where to find her, he didn't want to try his luck. After all, she'd been ready for him, knew his name, knew his . . . preferences. He'd been sold out and there was no reason to think that his last-choice scoundrels wouldn't just do the same. No. Good old-fashioned skulking would have to do.

His wristcom lit up and the anger drained back out of him. A hologram of a pair of smiling mephite women hovered above screen with the label MOM + MA. He considered rejecting the call, but the gnawing guilt made him answer.

"Hi, Mom," he said, the false cheer grating his own ears. There was rustling on the other end of the line as two women bickered back and forth.

"Haez, sweetie, is your video not working? We aren't seeing you."

He stared himself down in the reflection in the flexiglass behind his terminal. He could imagine the terror in his gentle mom's face if she were to see him like this. Ma would be worse. She would start planning vengeance.

"Yeah, something's wrong with my wristcom."

His ma's abrasive voice cut in, "Replace that hunk of junk. That job of yours should pay enough."

"Mm-hmm." Haez avoided talking about his "job" as much as he could. Technically, telling them he was working doing deliveries wasn't a lie. Still, staying coy about the nature of deliveries and his usual clientele was best to keep them from worrying. It was already hard enough to dodge the question of why he couldn't come home even for a few days.

It was just supposed to be a weekend away with friends for his twenty-fourth birthday, all of them stupidly eager to try their hand at oppos in a real casino rather than huddled around a kitchen table. None of them made it back to Ghusn. Before the end of their first night, Haez and his four closest friends had dug themselves deep into debt with the Sabres and were left with no choice but to sign their lives away. Six years later, all his friends had long since been eaten by Quantrin: dying by misadventure, killed by other gang members, or simply vanished like so many others. Haez was the last one standing again. Lucky him.

It was easier to say he was a busy courier rather than an indentured drug runner, just like it was easier to say that he and his friends had just grown apart. Their families deserved closure, and it destroyed him to know that he couldn't offer it—not without risking his own life. All it would take was one overzealous champion of justice to let Haez's name slip to a reporter, and Staukar would likely decide that he was too much trouble to keep around.

Quantrin was the perfect trap, and he wasn't the first overconfident loser to find it locked around him. Was that why Sonia was on the planet too? He didn't recall seeing a bracelet, but she had hidden *a lot* under that massive coat.

He didn't realize he'd been spacing out and staring at Sonia's record until his ma's voice cut through his thoughts. "Kid? Are you listening?"

"Sorry, Ma, just distracted."

"We were just wondering if you might be able to make it home for the holidays this year. Not that we don't appreciate the calls, but it would be nice to see you in person," his mom said, following a little hopefully. "Maybe with a girlfriend? Is that why you've been so busy?"

Even in the static mugshot, Sonia's eyes kept drawing him in, taunting him to come find her. "Maybe, Mom. I—"

His wristcom flashed again with another incoming transmission. Vrix. *Shit.* He rejected it as his parents whispered excitedly to each other.

"Look, I gotta go. I'll call you back when . . . when I'm coming home."

"Wait, Haez—"

He cut them off and paused to think for a moment before flying into motion. He didn't have much left for possessions: some clothes, a handful of flavourless kelp bars, a picture of his mothers. It all got shoved into his satchel and slung across his chest. After all, if Vrix thought he was dodging Staukar, it wouldn't take long before he showed up on Haez's doorstep to drag him in before he skipped town.

And skipping town needed to be an option.

If he couldn't track Sonia down, then there was no money and if Staukar didn't get his money . . . well, homeless was better than dead.

He left his unit for the last time, and after a moment of thought, he left the door open. The only thing remaining was his plants, and he could only hope that maybe someone would steal them for their own unit. The thought was more comforting than knowing that they would slowly shrivel and die without his attention.

With that, he left his residential block and set out across the rattling, drippy walkways. Sonia Jentis. Sonia fucking Jentis.

4

Sonia

The sounds of afternoon foot traffic wafted up through the open window of Sonia's unit. It was stuffed full of furniture—a wardrobe bulging with wigs and different outfits, tables scattered with shiny baubles and a cramped in-home gym. Sonia sat on a lumpy sofa well-past its prime but the idea of throwing away precious furniture still set her nerves on edge. Her datapad was propped up playing an old holodrama whose lead actress Sonia studied.

The woman looked too elegant to be real, and with every toss of her coiffed head, Sonia imitated it, imagining how to lengthen her neck and fake the natural grace of the actress. A week prior, Ottok had given her a tip that a wealthy politician had taken a shine to a nearby wine bar—just low-level enough to feel 'gritty and real' without having to actually look at the hungry faces of his constituents. A lonely heiress who knew the importance of discretion would be perfect to draw him in, and she already knew where to find the muse to build out her character.

It didn't hurt that this had been her grandmother's favourite program. The haughty countess on the screen was as familiar as an old friend, and Sonia only needed half an excuse to revisit her.

There was a banging knock at her door. Without looking away from the program, she said, "Come in," in a voice that had become deeper and smokier as she'd practiced the persona.

The door swished open to admit Ottok, laden down with bags and casting an appraising eye at her rehearsing. He grunted as he lifted them onto a table slightly too high for his short frame and took a seat on one of her mismatched chairs.

"You're getting better at that one. What's with the . . . " Ottok awkwardly mimicked Sonia's head-tossing. She paused the feed and pointed to the screen.

"See her lines?" she asked, tracing a finger from the top of the actress' head down to her shoulder. "It makes her look so poised. My neck isn't long enough, though. I'm going to have to talk to Finni at the shop and see if she has any tips for how to fake that." The proprietor of the cosmetics store a few towers away was fond of Sonia and business was usually slow enough that she was happy to show her how to use the product properly.

It was bittersweet to visit bubbly Finni. Her help is what let Sonia turn her hustle into an art form. Not that she could ever know that. As far as she knew, Sonia was a struggling actress named Gence who was just trying to make herself look good for auditions. If only that were true.

Ottok gave a nod to the video and turned his attention to the flex that was strewn out on a low table to his side. He pinched the top page between his talons and looked it over. "You got your entry plan memorized, then?" he asked with a skeptical glance.

"Yes," Sonia said, returning to her natural voice and turning off the program, "but you're going to quiz me anyways, aren't you?"

Ottok didn't acknowledge this, instead tracing a finger down the page.

"Which way do you go after getting off the tram?"

"South end," Sonia said, standing and stretching her spine, "staying on the main walks until platform 173. Then I take service lanes to avoid any home security cameras."

Ottok nodded before running his finger down and continuing, "And at the gate?"

"It's electrified. I use dampers to stop the current and climb before they get burnt off."

"Then at the security panels?"

Sonia walked around the couch to where Ottok was sitting, plucking the flex away from him. "I got it, Dad. Really. You brought the gear I need?"

He gave her a peevish look and gestured to the bulging bags on the table.

"Those have dampers, security spikes and a cutting torch. There's a facial static shield too if any cameras catch you, but don't rely on it."

Sonia nodded and crouched beside the low table. She pulled a page out of the mix and tapped at a few places on the plans. "Looks like three power supplies. How many spikes are in there?"

"Enough," Ottok said, grunting as he pulled himself out of his seat and waddled around to Sonia's side of the table. Standing next to her, he pointed to the windows on the plan. "You'll need to watch out for those. They're going to be double-sealed—physical and holo barriers. Barriers will be on a self-sustaining circuit. If you disrupt the circuit, you'll only have a minute to get the flexiglass out before they boot themselves up again. Any part of you that's in the frame when they reignite will be sliced through. It'll be tight. If you're not sure, back off until they restart and then short them out again."

The whole thing was going to be like defusing a house-sized bomb. Each power panel would have to be knocked out within seconds of each other. Otherwise, any that were still online would send an alert about the outage.

"Don't suppose you have a couple drones, do you?"

"I'll give you two if you stop calling me Dad."

"I can live with one," Sonia replied with a grin. Ottok sighed and dug around his personal bag to produce two fist-sized drones. *Big push-over,* she thought.

"I appreciate it, Ottok. Really. And hey, I-I was thinking," she said, shuffling her feet and awkwardly avoiding eye contact, "you know, if this is going to be as big a haul as we think, maybe I could help you with selling it off? Work on my negotiation skills?"

Ottok's ash-grey facial feathers contorted as his brow furrowed. "I don't think that's a good idea, kiddo."

"Come on, you can't be my only contact forever. I need to be able to sell by myself. I need to be able to get leads without you."

"The tourist hustle is your biggest earner. If anyone else gets wind that you're a player, you won't be able to get away with it anymore," Ottok said sternly. Sonia threw up her hands in frustration.

"Oh, no, I won't be able to get groped by drunk perverts. However will I cope?"

Ottok's feathers puffed around him like an angry cat. "Who groped you? Haez?"

"Oh, my god, no. He's literally the only one who didn't. I know it's a good earner, Ottok, but I don't like it. It makes me feel—"

Alone.

"—like a piece of meat. And if it goes well, it can be like a . . . coming-out job? No, that doesn't sound right. Look—"

"No, you look, Sonia," Ottok interrupted, worry written on his face, "I'm not saying you couldn't. You're a good burglar. Hell, a great one. But if you put yourself out there, then that's it. Your face will be known. You'll make enemies. You'll be stuck in this life, and I don't think you understand how lucky you are to have the option to walk away. Are you trying to tell me that *this* is what you want to do forever?"

She gave a bitter smile and sat back, picking at her cuticles. "I *already* have a record, Ottok. What else am I supposed to do? Work for Finni? Explain how Gence is actually Sonia and why she has a rap sheet? It's not like breaking and entering gets you a lot of transferable skills."

Ottok sighed and leaned back against the table beside her. He rubbed at a hoop piercing the bridge of his beak: the token taken on by gallans once they became elders. All gallan beak-piercings were received after major milestones. Ottok's beak was so encrusted with metal that what little beak remained was peeling and riddled with hairline cracks, mostly held together by more metal fused over top. The old man must have really been worried to be falling back on that particular nervous habit.

Finally, he said quietly, "I wouldn't be able to protect you anymore, Sonia."

She leaned over and bumped her shoulder against his. "I don't think you can bitch about me calling you Dad *and* be an overbearing control freak. Besides, you're not going to be around forever."

His feathers ruffled again, and he gave an offended scoff. "I'm old, not dead."

"Explain the smell, then."

Ottok glared at her and twisted around to take back the drones on the table. Sonia jumped up, raising her hands placatingly.

"Sorry, sorry, sorry, bad joke. I'm just asking you to think about it. Please? Until I get back?"

He grumbled and wagged a finger at her. "Just remember, fifty-fifty is the deal. Don't you go getting killed. And . . . we can talk about it when the job is done. No promises."

Sonia clapped gratefully and held her arms open for a hug. He sighed and gave her an awkward side-hug before trundling out the door. She tossed a compact rucksack on the table and started packing it with Ottok's supplies. As she dug into one of the bags left behind, she found a bundle of food bars at the bottom, all tied together with a note reading *stay safe*.

"Thanks, Dad," she whispered to herself, sliding the folio and food bars in before zipping the pack closed. All that was left were the clothes—black bodysuit, rubberized gloves, cargo belt, and emergency chute in case she got knocked off to a lower level. Going out the front door wouldn't do—not if she wanted to avoid any cameras. Instead, she disabled the holoshielding on her window frame and swung herself out. Her hands found the familiar fingerholds that she had used to get in and out a hundred times before. The burn in her arms and the feel of metal cutting into her fingertips shook the cobwebs out of her brain. By the time she had reached the walkway, her mind felt bright and clear and ready.

The walkway rattled as she thumped down, and a shiver went down her spine. Like someone was about to trace their fingers over the back of her neck. She whipped around and looked both ways down the lane.

Nothing. Just a bad feeling. Sonia shook her head, blaming the nerves.

She exited onto the main platform, melting into the end-of-day foot traffic and joining the river of people moving to the public transit terminals. Only the wealthy could justify a private glider in Quantrin's restrictive air traffic lanes. Everyone else waited for the snaking, multicar trams that traversed between levels. Even after all her years in the city, the sight of them always made Sonia think of flying earthworms.

Although the transit was public and went to all corners of every level, it all came with a price. The residents of the exclusive upper towers made a point to make it difficult for any of the riffraff to come sniffing around. Every level seemed to sneer with disgust at whatever level was right below them, no matter how far-down the towers they themselves resided.

Sonia had to get to the top without having her identity recorded by her tram pass, or her face captured on camera. One of the worm-gliders arced down to the terminal, slowing to a bobbing stop, and its dozen segments slid open, making the side all but vanish. While the transport authorities watched to ensure that everyone tapped their wristcoms against the ID readers, Sonia sidled up to the railing that blocked off the last bit of the glider's tail. She rocked on her heels like she was just waiting for a different route, and she watched.

At the last second, when the segments slid closed and latched into place, she hopped the fence and grabbed a handhold beside the emergency exit. If any of the transport authorities noticed her, it was too late for them to act before the glider departed. Her stomach lurched downwards as they began their ascent to the upper levels.

Getting between levels without being noticed was the easy part. She secured herself to the handhold as best she could so she could focus on settling her nerves before the hard part. With deep breaths, she relaxed her mind by focusing on her surroundings: the sunlight filtering through the layers of spiderwebbed walkways; the air get lighter as they rose; the shorter towers falling away and leaving enough space for wind to sneak its fingers through the endless pillars of synthsteel.

She just wished the bad feeling would ease up.

• • • • ● • ● • • • •

Sonia was able to hop off the worm-glider at the topmost levels early enough to see some of the lingering rays of pure sunlight before they disappeared behind the distant buildings of the city planet. She paused at the edge of a platform that faced towards the dying light. How long had it been since she had seen real sunlight that hadn't filtered down through the tiny gaps of sky visible from her usual levels? Even the air felt cleaner and warmer up here; no wonder rich people liked it.

Once the last sliver of sun vanished from sight, she was on the move again. Her and Ottok's careful planning paid off, with Sonia able to get to the manor leaving no more trace than a shadow. By the time she attached the dampers to the gate to flip herself over, she was starting to think this would go easier than expected.

Then she remembered the power panels.

"Come on, you little bastard," Sonia muttered to herself. She crouched behind the kind of lush shrubbery that could only exist on the sun-soaked upper levels. One of the drones bobbed and veered above drunkenly as Sonia fiddled with the controls on a display screen. The security spike strapped to its belly was throwing off the balance and making the delicate operation even more difficult.

She looked through the screen at the high-above power panel. For once, she felt like being a human was giving her an advantage. It looked like whoever lived here was human herself and must have had an affection for historical architecture. Unlike most units that were tucked inside whichever skyscraper supported them, the old lady had taken advantage of her rooftop real estate to build an actual *house*—an absurd indulgence in its own right. Moreover, it was the sort of ostentatious mansion that Sonia hadn't seen outside the historical dramas her grandmother had preferred. The security features were so beautifully integrated into the design that only a holodrama fiend like Sonia could have spotted the small inconsistencies that marked them.

The sucker couldn't have pulled this off if he tried, she thought, almost wishing she had been able to gloat at him a bit more.

Finally, the drone stabilized. Sonia lifted her hands away from the controls before she could mess up its delicate balance. After getting the second one stabilized, she took the third security spike in hand. With a quick tap on each of the screens, the drones were sent barreling forward, jamming their spikes through the protective panelling and into the delicate electronic innards. They both exploded into showers of sparks that sent the drones tumbling down, burnt-out and useless. Then she used all her strength to stab the last spike through the panel to her side before an alert could be sent.

She had to let go at the last second to avoid being burnt up like the drones. A crackle of electricity blistered her palm even through her gloves and her hair stood on end. Still, she was able to tumble back before any real damage was done. The electricity pulsed and sparked between the three panels like synapses short circuiting. After a moment, it fizzled out and the house went dark.

"Damn, I'm good," she whispered with a smile.

Compared to her close brush with electrocution, crawling up the side of the house to overload the window circuit and pushing in the flexiglass was easy. The holoshielding snapped to life behind her as she tumbled through the window and into a thickly carpeted hallway. She left the panel of flexiglass on the carpet and practically jumped over it to go down the corridor. She may have had all night, but she was far too eager to see if this house was as profitable as promised.

When she entered the massive lounge adjoining the hallway, her brain could hardly comprehend the wealth on display. Saying the old lady was rich was a comical understatement. The lush space was like a trail of candy, with every surface littered with some new bauble of increasing value. She hadn't even gotten to the really good stuff, and she was already filling her belt pouches with jewellery and trinkets. Just when she thought she had never seen so much money gathered in one place, she turned the corner.

The gallery. The centrepiece of the mansion. Sonia garbled speechlessly at the sight.

The walls were covered in art of unimaginable value and the floor space was peppered with enclosed display cases holding priceless antiques, statues, and more jewellery. Her brain glazed over at realisation that the pieces she had already collected were the cheap bits. Forget the coming-out job—she could retire off this.

Sonia unclipped a book-sized block from her belt and threw it down at the ground. With a popping sound, it unfurled into a hovercart large enough to hold four grown men and sturdy enough to hold up to a hasty getaway. After sparking a lightrod in the room, she got to work.

She loaded up the art first—that's where the real money was anyways. But once she was done, she couldn't resist taking some time with the jewellery. There was just something about pretty, shiny things that tickled her brain. The prettiest and shiniest was a sumptuous collar that formed a heavy, dripping cascade of gold and diamonds from her jaw to her breastbone. She snapped it around her neck and loosened the top of her jumpsuit so it could sit flush against her skin, with strands of opulence tickling over her shoulders and down her spine. Decadent. Absolutely decadent.

Maybe she would keep this one. It could never see the light of day, not as long as she lived on Quantrin. But maybe as a memento, something to wear when she indulged the imagination of a life beyond this. Maybe she could be like Gence one day. Hell, even like Finni.

There were a handful of paintings too big for the cart that still lined the wall, protected by shiny flexiglass. She sashayed in front of one of the frames, using the reflection to admire herself. Or tried, at least—the room was too dark to see properly. She brought the lightrod closer to see her reflection. The air rushed out of her lungs.

The mephite. Her mark stood behind her shoulder in the reflection, looking like a demon of rage and vengeance. Before she could get her breath back to scream, his hand slapped over her mouth and jerked her backwards into the darkness.

5

Haez

Sonia's body thumped back against Haez's chest and his mind was overwhelmed again with how nice she smelled. He had time to ruminate while he followed her up from her neighbourhood and breezed past the security features that she had helpfully disabled. When he was sparking a short into the holoshielding and letting her do the hard work of loading up the take, all he could think about was how good it was going to feel to finally choke the lights out of her. Now that her perfect body was pressed against him, his traitor brain flipped to wanting to bury his nose against her neck and find out if she tasted as good as she smelled.

Sonia struggled and squirmed against him, making his cock harden against her back despite the elbow she was trying to dig into his stomach. No matter how strong she was for a human, she was still dwarfed by his towering frame and couldn't break away. Haez pulled her tighter to him and hissed in her ear, "Did you miss me, pretty lady?"

To his surprise, Sonia whimpered and ground back against the bulge pushing into her mid back. There was some very small part of his brain that yelled at him that this wasn't the plan, and to not to trust any of this, but it was overwhelmed by the smell and feel of her. He groaned deeply and yanked the jewelled collar off her body to give him access to her throat. Haez's hand slid down from her mouth to grip her jaw and arch her head away, showing off the smooth expanse of her soft golden skin. He pressed his nose to the space between her neck and shoulder and breathed her deep. When his tongue flicked out to taste her skin, she moaned and snuck a hand up to caress the back of his scalp, holding him in place. She tasted even better than he'd imagined. Soon he was drunk off her, kissing and nipping bruises across her throat and shoulder.

"No," she panted, smiling devilishly, "but I didn't know you had this in you. You seemed like such a big softy in the bar."

"Maybe I am for scared little birds. That's not you, though, is it, *Sonia?*"

She startled at the sound of her name but seemed to mentally file it for later as her body melted back against his. She arched her head backwards to look up at him, her lips parted slightly and showing just a peek of pink tongue.

"Is that what you like? I could do that for you, baby. I could do so much for you," she whispered, letting her tongue run over her lips.

Something in Haez snapped. He spun Sonia around to face him and crushed his lips to hers in a bruising kiss, slicking his tongue over hers. She tried to kiss him back, craning her neck painfully to stretch up towards him. It only took a minute before Haez became frustrated hunching over her. He bent his knees and scooped her up against him, hands spanning her ass and grinding himself fully into her hot centre. She gave more of those pathetic whines as she clung to him, pushing against his cock, as desperate for him as he was for her.

Haez sat her down on a cabinet and let his hands roam her body. Did he think she was beautiful before when she was playing at being a fragile tourist? It was nothing compared to how she felt now, all hard muscle rolling under his fingertips. Before, she was a flickering candle on the verge of burning out—now, she felt like an inferno on his tongue. He let a finger trace over a stiffening nipple through her jumpsuit.

"Tell me," he gasped. "Tell me what you can do for me."

Sonia's hands jumped to her collar and yanked the zipper down as far as it would go. When she started trying to shimmy out of the sleeves, Haez gave an impatient growl, gripping either side of the garment and ripping it open along the seam running between her thighs. She leaned back into him, pulling at his lower lip with her teeth while her hands fumbled his belt open. Haez gave a startled moan when she reached in to squeeze his length, humming appreciatively.

"You're big all over, huh?" she breathed. "If I knew you were packing this, maybe I would have gotten you to take me home."

Haez pulled his head back and stared at her incredulously, fury in his eyes. "Do you think this is a fucking joke?"

Unblinking, she sneered, "I think *you* are."

Haez gritted his teeth and shoved his pants down enough to free his cock. He planted one of his hands over her throat and squeezed, roughly shoving her head back against the wall behind the cabinet.

"Shut up. Shut the fuck up, you little brat," he snarled at her. Her eyes glittered with excitement as she smiled at him.

"What if I don't?" She tilted her head back ever-so-slightly so his hand could wrap more fully around her neck. Even as enraged as he was, Haez's eyes flicked to Sonia's face, looking for any sign of fear or nerves. She held his gaze and gave him another small smile and a nod.

He took his cock in hand and lined it up against her already-dripping cunt, sliding the head through the slick to tease her clit. But only for a second—he didn't feel like giving her the benefit of foreplay. As he tightened his grip on her throat, he slammed into her in one stroke.

Sonia's eyes went wide and a strangled cry forced its way out of her before being cut off by Haez's grip. It stroked his ego, seeing the way her legs quivered helplessly and how every thrust he pounded into her seemed to knock the air out of her lungs. Together with watching how her body had to stretch to its limits to take his dark-red length, he was nearly feral with lust.

He purred when he leaned into her ear, "Is this what you wanted last night? Did you want me to catch you after you left the bar? I bet you wanted me to bend you over and fuck the sass right out of you."

She clenched around him and let out a guttural moan at his filthy talk. He grinned and continued, "You like that, don't you? You like me ruining your little human cunt with this big mephite cock? You can't even talk, can you, you cock-dumb slut."

Sonia's throat made a gulping sound. Haez eased his hand to let her speak. When he did, she gave a mocking smile and gasped, "That's all . . . you got?"

Haez felt rage cut back through his lust. He pulled out of her and jerked her off the cabinet by her upper arm, planning to bend her over and show her just how punishing he could be. Once Sonia got her feet on the ground, though, she grabbed him by his coat and used his own momentum to send him tumbling to the ground. Before he could get his feet back under him, she straddled him and rubbed herself against his length, taking her own pleasure from his body.

When he realized that she wasn't trying to kill him, Haez relaxed back against the floor and enjoyed the sight of Sonia grinding her clit on him. He reached up and jerked the split fabric of her jumpsuit farther open, letting her tits bounce out for him to palm. He pinched and rolled her nipples between his fingers, making her whine and falter in her motions.

"What's the matter, Sonia? Don't think you can handle riding it?"

Before she could reply, he spanked her hard enough to make her yelp. He growled at her, "Ride. It."

Sonia didn't argue—just lifted herself, lined up his cock, and dropped down. When she bottomed out, she paused and panted, "Fuck. Oh, fuck, fuck, fuck."

Haez flexed his cock inside her and smiled smugly when even that small motion sent more tremors through her. He slapped her ass again and rolled her hips down onto him.

She rode him hard, grinding her clit into him every time she rocked back and forth. The only sounds she could manage were choked whimpers and squeaks, even as dirty talk rolled out of Haez as smoothly as oil. He told her what a tight little cock-sleeve she was, how he wanted to fuck her right on the bar so all the other patrons could see how good she looked stuffed with his cock, how she was going to be crawling back to him begging to be his fuck toy. Every word sent another rush of slick to her core and spurred her to ride faster.

It didn't take long before Sonia tensed and froze above him. Just as he was going to spank her again to get her moving, her pussy clenched around him and she let out a keening wail. It broke down any restraint Haez had left. He gripped her hips tight to hold her in place and pounded up into her, treating her like nothing more than a wet hole for his enjoyment.

His end wasn't far behind. When he finally broke, he slammed himself deep inside her one last time and held her pressed tightly to him groaning, "Take it. Fucking take it."

He held her there for a minute as the last tremors of his orgasm rattled through him. Sonia had gone boneless. She collapsed against his chest, both of them panting and lost in the afterglow of the brutal fucking. After a few minutes of rest, Sonia lifted her head from his chest and looked at his face with a blissfully dazed expression. She let her hand trail over his horns, his gaunt features, his pointed ears. He almost missed her grazing down towards the gun on his belt.

He snatched her hand away and held it aloft. In a flash, her eyes turned wide and furious, and she reeled back with her other fist. Before she could land a hit, Haez knocked her off him and flat onto her back. She punched and kicked at him as he dragged her by her wrist to a banister, meanwhile unclipping a pair of binders from the other side of his belt.

"Bet you thought you were really cute, didn't you? Thought you could just push your tits out and squirm out of this one too?" Haez snarled. He snapped the binders around her wrists, securing her in place. Sonia kicked out at him again, but he jumped back just in time to avoid any damage to his still-exposed cock.

"It's just business. It's not my fault you're such an easy mark. You're taking this so personally."

He scoffed and glared down at her. "You want to see taking it personally? We'll see how understanding the owner of this place is when she finds you locked up here and her entire collection cleared out. Try fucking your way out of that one."

Sonia rolled her eyes and slumped back against the banister. She didn't stop glaring at him as he tucked himself away and went to check the hovercart. It was half-filled with lots of room for the little pieces she was fawning over. *What the hell,* he thought. *We have time.*

"So, tell me, Sonia Jentis," he hollered, picking up where she left off loading the chest, "since we have so much time to get to know each other, I am curious; Which one was it that sold me out to you?"

She scoffed, "No way I'm telling you. Some of us actually have a sense of loyalty to the people who help us out."

"What, are you scared I'm going to run to the cops? I'll tattle while they book me. Come on, live a little. Rub my nose in it."

Her mouth pursed a little before she spat, "It was Ottok. Did you really think he was going to help you out again? Your last stunt nearly put him out of business."

He tried not to show how much that answer stung. It was Ottok who showed Haez the ropes when he first fell under contract to Staukar. The Sabres couldn't have cared less if he lived or died as long as his deliveries were completed. He owed Ottok a lot. Learning how badly he had soured their friendship had been like a splash of ice water. "It sounds like you're the one taking it personally now," he said, tossing another gaudy, golden trinket in with the rest. "Are you one of his strays? I thought I knew everyone Ottok looked after, but I've never seen you around."

"I'm new in town."

Now he had to laugh. "No, you're not. I saw your record. You've been getting in trouble here for at least seven cycles."

"No," she said, putting on the breathy little-bird voice she used back at the bar, "I'm just a lost widdle student who just needs someone to care what happens to her." She dropped back to her natural voice. "Ottok told me a little about you. And your weird fetish."

"It's not—" He had to smack a hand against a wall to catch himself before his temper got the better of him. A few deep breaths got his voice level, but he could still feel his cheeks burning. He wiped his hand down his face before replying. "I don't have a fetish. I've never even . . . been with a human before now. I was just a little drunk and mentioned to Ottok that some of them—you people—were . . . attractive."

"Yeah, I could tell how 'attractive' you thought I was."

Haez wanted to scoff and put her in her place, but the sight of her on the ground, clothes ripped open and white dribbling out of her and onto the carpet made his mouth go dry. He pinned her with a heated look. "I didn't hear you complaining."

Her bravado faltered under his stare, and she pinched her knees together like she was suddenly shy. She gave a too-casual shrug and stammered, "I-It could have been better."

Haez smirked and nodded at her flustered response. "Right. So, you make your money bilking sorry assholes like me. I'm guessing Ottok put you onto that angle too. How'd you even end up on Quantrin?"

Her jaw tightened and she looked away. "It's . . . complicated."

He studied her suddenly guarded reaction. Stripping away the sass and swagger, she was pretty young. Seven years ago would have made her a kid, and that was just when she'd started hustling. If she got stuck here, it's because someone had stopped taking care of her.

He didn't press further. Some wounds didn't need more salt.

"I've heard about you too, you know," she said. "Haez Coubik, the piss-poor drug-runner who can't stay out of the casinos long enough to make sure he finishes a job? You got a real way with people, baby.

The way I hear it, there isn't anyone left on Quantrin that you haven't managed piss off. No idea why anyone gave you a job this good."

He paused. She snorted victoriously, like she'd managed to wound his self-esteem. But that wasn't it. The problem was that she was right. No matter how expensive or impossible it would have been to pull this one off, it was still too big of a take to give away to anyone he didn't like. The Delnuls might not have hated him, but they certainly didn't have any reason to like him.

That meant there was a catch.

Sonia's snide smile flickered at the sudden alarm on Haez's face. "What is it?"

"Do you have the folio on you?"

Sonia furrowed her brows and pulled her head back, confused by his reaction. "It's in my bag. Why?"

He dove in and started frantically flipping through the flex, looking for any clues. "Do you remember the name of the lady who owns this place?"

She shook her head. "No. It wasn't listed."

"You're sure?"

She gave him an annoyed nod. He started tearing through the living area, looking for some other clue. He found one in the collection of framed photos on the mantle.

His blood ran cold.

It wasn't about who the lady was. It was about who she knew. Nearly all the photos featured a sharp-featured, elderly woman smiling graciously at the camera and just as many contained a familiar, cold-eyed face.

Staukar. Not just adult photos, either. Some of them had a hawkish little boy who would unmistakably grow into his former employer.

This place belonged to Staukar's mom. The most powerful and ruthless crime boss on the planet, and Haez was in his mother's living room with a chest loaded with her most prized possessions. Did he think he was dead before? He may as well have never existed.

Right on cue to make a bad situation terminal, the household lights flicked on, and from downstairs came the sound of the front door sliding open.

Without thinking, Haez crouched and held his breath. Even Sonia knew well-enough to keep her smart mouth shut. She leaned towards him and hissed, "I thought she was supposed to be gone the whole weekend."

"Well, you said it. No one likes me this much." He scuttled toward the cart and tapped a couple buttons to send it floating towards the hallway and the breached window. Sonia struggled against the cuffs, looking from him to the noises downstairs.

"Are you seriously still going to leave me here? We can just dump it and go," she whispered shakily.

"What else do I do? I'm dead no matter what. Even if we leave everything behind, Staukar is still going to know that someone broke into his mom's house, and my money says the Delnuls are ready to get into his good graces by letting him know who had the place marked. If I can get money, I can at least get off world. If he wants to kill me, the bastard is gonna work for it." He was about to leave the lounge when Sonia's voice went very small.

"Staukar?"

He looked back at her. All the blood had drained from her face, leaving her sickly-white. The binders on her wrists trembled quietly with the rest of her body.

"Does Staukar know you?" Haez asked. Sonia shook her head and swallowed.

"I just know that Ottok said to never cross him. W-what will happen to me?"

She would be killed. He knew that as well as anyone. Even worse, if he left her looking like this, half-naked and dripping with an accomplice's cum, the death wouldn't be the first or worst thing to happen to her. It would buy him some time to get off planet while they ripped her apart, but the idea of her suffering on his account still left a bad taste in his mouth.

Haez was a screwup, not a monster.

He rushed back to her and fiddled with the binders. "You're a pain in my ass, Sonia Jentis," he muttered. Sonia let out a held breath in a rush. The binders unclicked and she rubbed the feeling back into her hands.

"Thank you," she breathed. "Thank you, Haez."

Sonia's wide and watery eyes made his chest tighten. She looked at him like he was something special and not just the worthless loser who almost left her to die. He didn't deserve it, but that didn't stop him from wanting it as much as he wanted another taste of her skin.

Thumping steps on the stairs from the opposite hallway snapped them back to their dire reality. "Come on," he whispered, pulling her up by the elbow. She was a step ahead of him, darting out the door they entered through and away from the footsteps. She sent a spark of electricity into the circuitry around the frame to make the shielding drop. It died with a fizzle, and they pushed the cart through, letting it float gently downwards. Haez shoved her through next. She didn't need any more encouragement and swung out to crawl down the wall, quick as a llozal.

The footsteps grew closer. Haez didn't have time for grace as he hurled himself through the frame and onto the filled chest just in time to hear the holoshielding buzz back on behind him. Sonia followed his lead and jumped off the wall, thumping into the cart. The motors in the delicate frame groaned under their combined weight. In seconds, it rebounded off the ground. The contents were rattled but undamaged.

"Where do we go now?" she asked as she climbed off the cart, with barely suppressed panic crackling her voice and quickening her breath.

"Down," he said, "down as far as we can go before they start searching."

Haez pushed the cart towards the railing enclosing the edge of the skyscraper. With an angry whir, the motors strained to hover over the railing and the cart floated out over the abyss. He extended a hand to Sonia.

"After you, pretty lady."

The exhausted twitch of a smile on her face eased Haez's anxiety. She would be back to sassing him soon enough. For now, she was thankfully compliant, taking his hand and letting him help her onto the cart. They both winced at the sound the contents made as she tried to wedge herself in-place. Once she was secure, he took a spot beside her and, untethered and praying, sent them and their spoils drifting down into the darkness.

6

Sonia

It took hours of floating downward, pressing themselves as low as possible whenever they drifted by any windows and with Haez occasionally steering to slip between walkways so they could get a little deeper into the city. When they were between the layers of walkways, Sonia did her best to dig clothes out of his pack to replace her ruined ones. Everything was too big, having to belt the pants tightly and roll the cuffs halfway up the legs. It still beat walking around with her pussy hanging out. She used the ruins of her jumpsuit to clean herself off before tossing them off into the depths.

When their eyes became too bleary to continue, Haez guided the cart to an empty platform. It rebounded gently off the metal and he jumped out first, still coursing with enough adrenaline to land solidly and quickly scan their surroundings. Satisfied that there were no witnesses, he turned back to Sonia and helped her stumble down from the cart.

She wrinkled her nose at the wet-dog smell that permeated their surroundings. The constant dripping of the higher levels was replaced by steady rivers of mystery fluids digging trenches into mildewy metal walls. Not enough of the anemic sunlight could reach down to dry away the damp, and the towers were too close-set to allow wind to carry away the stink. The rusted-away patches of walkways re-minded her to watch where they stepped.

Sonia hadn't been this deep in the city before. Part of Ottok's rules of survival had warned her way from these levels, which were home to the seedy brothels and gambling dens that made up the real backbone of Quantrin's economy. Humans, and especially human women, stuck to the higher levels that were accessible by spaceport—the safe, law-abiding levels. The only other humans she was liable to see were the girls working in Staukar's many establishments. If not that, the Ozarla fail sons that Staukar gave pity jobs to as part of his off-world business ventures.

That was another of Ottok's rules of survival: Do not fuck about with Mr. Staukar. The 'why' didn't matter—just the in-tensity of the warning was enough for Sonia.

She stuck close to Haez's side as they pushed the cart through empty back lanes that ringed abandoned industrial blocks. His coat was thrown over the top of the cart and Sonia stayed tucked under his arm, both to keep warm and to try to hide her face from anyone who might be too curious about a stray human. Under different circumstances, she would have been embarrassed. Her pride wouldn't allow for anyone to take care of her but herself, and for her protector to be *this* jerk? Intolerable.

At least he had taken a break from sniffing her. She wasn't sure if that was a mephite thing, a Haez thing, or if she just needed to reassess her grooming. Probably not the last one given how ravenous he had been for her. The thought of their intimacy raised the nagging worry of if humans and mephites were similar enough for their actions to have unplanned consequences.

There was enough to worry about without adding that to her mind. For now, she focused on his comforting hand on her shoulder and his body heat, which chased away some of her trembling.

Sonia had come close to dying before. She had slipped off walls, been thrown between levels, and had even been hit with a laser bolt or two that had to be stitched up by Ottok. This was different. It wouldn't have been a few hours of having a friend trying to save her before she drifted off into the forever sleep. If what she'd heard about Staukar were true, it would've been weeks of having pieces carved off of her until there wasn't anything left to slice. If they believed she could be used to draw Haez out, it probably would have been even worse.

If he hadn't been there to piece things together, she would have gone waltzing back to Ottok and started advertising to every other crook in the city about her impressive haul—maybe even selling it personally, if Ottok had let her. *I'm so stupid,* she thought. *A stupid, stupid, little human wanting to prove she's a big-time burglar.* Suddenly, she really felt like the nervous little girl she'd played in the bar. Sensing her tension, Haez drew her in closer and brought his hand to the side of her head to talk quietly down to her.

"We're going to a motel. They're discreet and don't need ID. We've just eloped and we're looking for a cheap honeymoon that your parents won't find out about. I can do all the talking—you just need to act like a shy runaway. We hide the cart in the alley and sneak it in after we have a room key. Can you handle that?"

She nodded firmly. There was a plan. Haez had a plan. They just had to stick to the plan, and they'd be okay.

Everything is going to be okay.

· · · ● · ● · ● ● · · ·

Being able to focus her attention on a plan helped soothe her frayed nerves. She clung to it like an anchor in a stormy sea. When they found a few dumpsters to hide the cart behind, she took his jacket from the top and slung it on. Borrowing a hand-mirror from the cart, she looked at herself and arranged the coat to dwarf herself as much as possible. Simultaneously, she ran her role over in her head: young enough to be easily swooned by an older man, but not so young that it grossed her out; shy and inexperienced, but trying her hardest to be appealing to her seasoned husband; naïve, pitiable, and too stupid to know it.

As she thought on this, she watched her own face and honed how she would carry herself as this new person. Haez appeared over her shoulder in the mirror, his ruby nose wrinkled with distaste.

"Fuck, that's weird," he said. Her lips pursed with annoyance, and she turned back to him, character lost.

"Do not do that," she said, her hard stare and cold voice making it sound like a threat. "If you want this to be the story that we tell, you need to let me do my part for telling it. That means you need to let me get into character, and from this point on, you need to treat me like that character."

"Character? I told you I would talk. How hard is it to look shy?"

Sonia breathed deep through her nose and counted silently back from ten. "'Shy' doesn't make an entire person. Do you even know who you're going to pretend to be?"

Haez threw up his hands in frustration and huffed back, "I don't know. An asshole."

Turning away from him to look back at the mirror, Sonia muttered under her breath, "Not much of an act."

"Wait, do you do this whenever you scam someone? How long were you doing it before you ambushed me at the bar?"

"Before I left my unit. Now can you shut the fuck up?"

Haes scoffed and shook his head but stayed mercifully quiet. She fell back into the same motions until her new skin settled. When she turned back to Haez, it was with a shy smile as she wrapped both hands around his forearm. He grimaced but didn't comment further, instead sliding his arm free and taking her hand. He jerked her behind him and dragged her away from the dumpster and along the side of the tower. Around the corner on the far end was a parking platform facing towards double-stacked rows of converted residential units. The door closest to them was bordered by large flexiglass windows and emitted a dingy orange light.

Right before they rounded the corner, Haez draped his arm over her shoulder and laughed loudly. Beside the lobby window, he suddenly pushed Sonia up against the wall. He leaned in hard and started devouring her mouth, tongue slicking against hers with deep throated moans. She was startled silent by the sudden act, and it took a moment before she reciprocated, whimpering into his mouth. His hand raked through her hair and yanked it back, forcing her neck to crane and her back to arch into him. It had her breathing hard and deaf to anything besides their heaving breaths and her own thunderous heartbeat. She could barely gather her thoughts enough to wrap her hands around his back, the feel of tight muscles flexing under his thin shirt sending shivers through her.

And as abruptly as it started, it stopped. Haez pulled away and left her slumped and panting against the wall. Sonia felt a wave of embarrassment wash over her, now acutely aware of the very real arousal slicking her upper thighs.

Get it together, Sonia. It's just an act like any other you've put on. Put your pussy in your pocket and move on, she thought. Haez grinned and hauled her back to his side to guide her into the lobby.

The door swished open to reveal a grungy, mildew-scented lobby, lined with a mismatched collection of tattered chairs and a water-stained desk. Behind the desk was a visibly bored litto, its segmented, caterpillar-like body propped up on a squeaking stool as it browsed something on a datapad held in one of its many hands. It gave them a glance and rolled its eyes as they approached. From where it was sitting, it would've had a prime view of their display outside, and clearly wasn't impressed. Haez leaned over the counter, still wearing the same punchable grin.

"Hey there, handsome. You been busy tonight?"

The receptionist gave him a flat stare and tapped around its datapad, ignoring the question. "A hundred credits a night or twenty an hour. What do you need?"

Haez leaned in conspiratorially. "Well, it's actually our honeymoon. How many nights can you do for us?"

"As long as you can pay, you can stay." The litto sent a judging eye at Haez's damaged horn, bruised face and damp, dirty clothes. "You *can* pay, right?"

Haez grinned and jingled a heavily-jewelled bracelet from the haul. The litto's face brightened at the sight of more money than it likely made in a cycle. "My wife's family is very generous. You give us a week and it's yours."

It reached out for the bracelet, but Haez jerked it back at the last second and added, "Also, if anyone comes asking, you never saw us.

Her brothers don't like me, and I don't want us to be interrupted, if you catch my drift." He added a greasy wink for good measure.

The litto's eyes narrowed and it peered around Haez to look at Sonia. She gave a flirtatious giggle, clung to Haez's arm, and simpered, "Whatever Daddy thinks is best." His face gave the smallest twitch and Sonia was able to hear a tiny, disgusted gag click in his throat. *That's how you perform, you amateur,* she thought, quietly pleased at Haez's discomfort. The receptionist either didn't notice or didn't care, turning back to its holopad and tapping in a room booking.

"Room 32 is yours for the next week, Mr. and Mrs. Hullek," it said, extending a hand for the bracelet. Haez dropped the prize in its palm and took the key card that was slid across the counter, using it to give a small salute before steering Sonia out of the lobby and alongside the lower exterior doors.

She didn't need to be playing a character to feel embarrassed about the lascivious moans and cries echoing through the doors of the neighbouring rooms. Hopefully the fact that they were staying for more than a few hours wasn't uncommon enough to set off suspicion. Haez didn't seem to notice, with his grin dropping the moment they left the lobby and replaced with a clenched jaw and twitchy eyes. He paused in front of their door and gave a last furtive look around the glider lot before opening it and gently pushing Sonia inside.

"Just wait here," he said quietly. "I'll be right back."

She gave him a nod and the door swished shut behind him. She turned to take in their temporary home. The room was washed in sickly orange lighting, making the grimy walls and threadbare bed look even crustier. She didn't even need to look in the bathroom to know that it was perpetually damp; the powdery grey mould creeping from that doorway onto the roof was enough of a tell.

It looked like safety. It looked like the most beautiful room she had ever seen in her life. She sat on the edge of the sagging bed and started peeling away damp layers of clothing. Haez's clothes. It was hard to believe that just that morning, she'd been hassling Ottok for extra drones and planning to be back before the noodle place under her unit closed.

Her unit. It hit her all at once that she would never see it again. Every hoarded possession and all the tiny mementos from her life before Quantrin would be stuffed in a dumpster or thrown off a walkway like the rest of the garbage that rained through the city. That sole island of stability and home had just vanished over the horizon. Her eyes welled up as she stared at the heap of soggy fabric on the ground.

I don't even have my own clothes.

There was the soft swish of the door sliding open again and Sonia quickly wiped away the tears before they could fall. Haez shoved the cart inside and shut the door behind him, collapsing back against the wall with a ragged breath of relief. He barely spared Sonia's half-naked body a glance as he walked to the opposite corner of the bed, slumped down, and followed her lead of shrugging off the sweat-stained clothes.

Sonia gathered up the heap that she left on the ground and began hanging the coverings over the edge of the cart, carefully facing away from Haez. "So, what now?" she asked over her shoulder.

"I don't know."

His voice sounded so defeated that Sonia turned to look at him. He was scrubbing a hand over his eyes like if he rubbed away the sleepiness, this would all turn out to be a bad dream. He continued, "I really wish I did, Sonia. But I don't."

"Well, we have a week, right?" Sonia replied, trying to summon some of the false calm that Haez had been projecting for hours. "You need to sleep. We both do. We can figure it out in the morning."

She pulled back the stiff covers on the bed and gestured for him to climb in. He gave a tired glance from the bed to her face.

"I can take the couch."

"You can. But you won't. We both need to get real sleep."

He opened his mouth to argue but was too exhausted to get the first word out. He muttered a half-hearted agreement and crawled under the covers, hugging the edge of the bed facing away from Sonia. It only took seconds for him to start snoring.

She watched enviously as the tension bled out of his body. She promised herself that she would sleep. First, she needed a shower.

7

Haez

Haez slept for what felt like an eternity. Once the adrenaline of the escape had worn off, his body had all but collapsed in their safe haven. When the faint background chatter of a news broadcast pushed through his sleep, he jerked awake.

Sonia startled from where she sat, curled into a lounge chair watching the holoscreen. His stomach dropped when he recognized the outside of Mama Staukar's estate, swarming with law enforcement.

"They haven't named any suspects," Sonia said.

"They won't. Staukar won't tell the cops," Haez replied grimly.

She gave a humourless smirk. "Any chance he might let it go?"

Even through her façade of cynicism, Haez didn't miss the hint of hopefulness in her tone. He was struck again by how young she could seem. He shook his head slowly, hoping she would understand the meaning behind it. Staukar wouldn't tell the cops because then the cops would care about what happened to them. Whatever Rakir was playing at, there was no way he hadn't passed on the information. Bastard was probably getting a pat on the head for being such a loyal little dog.

No, the only thing the news report confirmed was that going underground had been the right choice. If they had waited any longer, they might have disappeared already.

Sonia sighed deeply and turned off the holoscreen, turning to face Haez. "Didn't think so. We need to avoid him, then. How the hell are we going to do that on this level? Half the people down here work for him and the other half wishes they did."

"We can try getting farther down," Haez suggested. A revolted shudder swept over Sonia at the thought.

"No. I don't want to go deeper. I don't even like it here."

"Off-planet then. You might be able to hide out on the far-side of Quantrin, but I don't know if you'd want to chance it. Hells if I know where we'll find a transport willing to smuggle both of us though," Haez sighed, rubbing a hand over his browbone.

"What about Ottok?"

Haez shot Sonia a look and noticed that she was nervously fiddling with her wristcom, twisting it back and forth on its strap.

"Did anyone besides Ottok know about you stealing the plans?" When she shook her head, Haez let out a relieved sigh. "You can't call him, at least not until the heat dies down. He's survived this planet for a long time. He'll know to keep his mouth shut and let me take the heat. If you call, you're putting a target on you both."

"He could help us though. He knows everyone—probably someone who could transport us," she protested weakly.

"Come on, Sonia. You're smarter than that."

She gave him a dirty look and went silent. At that moment, Haez's stomach decided to make its presence known with a loud growl. Sonia gave a little smile.

"I think there's a vending machine around the corner."

"Sounds like a perfect breakfast. You're buying."

· · · ● · ● · ● · · ·

The stale pastries and childhood snacks scattered over the grimy bed helped chase away the sense of doom. The news broadcast had given way to a steady stream of children's shows neither of them were young enough to recognize. As long as they didn't look at the covered cart in the corner, it was almost nice.

Sonia was returning to normal as well. Her thick shoulders had relaxed into a loose hunch as she sat cross-legged on the bed. A stick of candied something dangled from her teeth as she made notes on the back of the flex from the folio.

"So, the way I see it," she said while gnawing the confection, "we need a transport, but we're going to have to rustle up some credits. If Staukar has been spreading the word, no one is going to touch any of our haul."

Haez interrupted her with a hum while he swallowed a mouthful of questionable meat bun. "Not the big stuff, sure. What about the jewellery? Most of it wasn't even locked up."

"Will that get us enough? Shit, Ottok always fenced for me. I don't even know how much to ask for that stuff."

Haez unfolded himself from the bed and went to check the cart. He pulled out the smaller items that Sonia had plucked up and spread them out on top of a dresser. He shook his head at the lineup.

"Not enough. Not even close." Haez stared thoughtfully at the jewellery, then flicked his stare to Sonia. She narrowed her eyes at him.

"What?"

"There *is* a way to turn a little money into a lot of money."

Sonia picked up an unopened candy bar and threw it at Haez's head. "I'm not hooking, you ass!"

The snack bounced harmlessly off Haez's face. He gave an exasperated sigh, retrieved it from the ground and opened it for himself. "I know we don't know each other that well yet, but I would never bully a woman into selling herself like that. Especially not you."

"What do you mean 'especially not me'?"

"Have you met you? I wouldn't live long enough to turn a profit."

Sonia snorted out a laugh, accidentally dropping a piece of food from her mouth. Her hand darted up to try to catch it and put it back into her mouth without Haez noticing. She failed and slapped it across the room.

And Haez noticed. As he watched her awkward flailing, his heart skipped a beat at how cute she could be when she was just being Sonia. His face heated and he cleared his throat. "I meant betting. There's a rixie circuit on this level. If we can sell a little of this, I can keep a low profile and place some bets."

Sonia lay back on the bed and stared at the ceiling, deep in thought. After a minute, she said, "So, I'm Staukar. I'm looking for a guy who just robbed my mom. I'm sending out every crook who wants a sniff of my asshole to find him. I know he's a big, red mephite with a busted horn, no buccal fat, and a gambling problem. What do they look for?"

She sat back up and looked at Haez. "I look for some big, red mephite with a busted horn and no buccal fat skulking around the track with his hood up. I look for someone who doesn't want to be seen in a place where he can indulge his issue without being noticed. You, sir, are going to get us killed if you do that."

"What's buccal fat?"

"You *would* ask that."

Haez rubbed a finger over his temple, trying to stave off an impending headache. "Fine, no racetracks. Any other suggestions?"

Sonia grinned and pointed her candy stick at him. "Casino."

Haez rubbed at his temple a bit harder.

"They're all owned by Staukar down here. Do you have any suggestions that aren't objectively stupider than the rixies?"

"That's the point."

Haez went silent to let her continue while wondering if he should be double-checking the expiration dates on their food. Sonia unfolded herself from sitting and started pacing as she spoke, getting more and more excited.

"Obviously, going to a casino owned by the man who's after your neck is suicidal. No sane person would do it. So why would anyone even bother looking for you there? It's perfect. We dress you up like you're some hot-shot and I'm your escort. You get the money, I get the information, and we're off the planet before he even knows we were on this level." She clapped her hands together and held them apart like she was expecting applause. Haez didn't provide.

"So, your idea is instead of having my hood up somewhere discreet, I march my big red mephite self with a busted horn and no . . . "

"Buccal fat."

" . . . that. I march into the heart of Staukar's operation and try to take *more* of his money."

"I'm not telling you to steal his wallet. You're a gambler, right? You must know how to hustle a card table."

Haez considered this. Frustrating as she could be, she wasn't wrong. It would be the last place someone would think to look for him, and he wasn't half-bad at playing oppos. For as much as he lost while gambling, he usually had good luck—until he didn't. He wasn't sure if he wanted to pin their chances on his ability to quit while he was ahead. But when Sonia said it, the whole insane scheme almost sounded possible.

Sonia must have sensed he was opening up to the idea because she interjected, "And you don't have to look like you. I don't want to brag—"

"Yes, you do."

"Yes, I do. I'm very good with makeup. Give me an hour to go find supplies and you'll be a brand-new mephite."

Haez let out a heavy sigh. "This is so fucking stupid."

Sonia gave him a wide grin, practically bouncing with excitement. "All the best plans are. Now these . . . " She pointed to the jewellery spread out over the dresser. "How much do I ask for these if I pawn them?"

Haez hemmed and hawed for a moment. "Pretend you're a rich guy's side piece that just learned about the wife and is selling all the gifts he gave you. They'll undercut you hard but shouldn't question it. Don't take less than eight thousand, though."

Sonia nodded and swept the jewellery into a satchel. Before leaving, she rifled through Haez's pack and tried to put together something to sell her character. She ended up settling on an oversized shirt that she belted into a pseudo-dress. Finally, she turned to a mirror and practiced her facial expressions, trying to master her new character before walking out the door. Haez shuddered. Watching in real-time as her personality melted off her face to be replaced by a stranger's was still as disconcerting as it was impressive.

When she was satisfied, she slung the satchel across her body and swept from the room without another word. Haez slumped onto the bed. Not much to do but enjoy the kids' shows until she returned.

Hopefully this stupid scheme wouldn't be the last thing he did.

· · · · ● · ● ● · · ·

Haez started to worry when one hour rolled into two. He was furious at himself for letting her go alone. What if someone else knew that she was in on the theft after all? What if someone recognized the jewellery? Hells, what if someone who just didn't like humans decided that the uppity mistress wandering alone needed to be taught a lesson? The last one made him clench his fists hard enough for his nails to cut into his palms. He didn't like the thought of anyone putting their hands on her.

No one but me.

He shook the thought away and scolded himself internally. Every affection she had shown him was an act. Even when she rode his cock like she needed it to live, it was a means to an end. But he was certain there was no lie in the way her eyes rolled back when he was inside her.

Just as he was wondering if he needed to go jerk off to clear his mind, the door slid open. Sonia nearly fell into the room, overloaded with bags. Haez rushed over to relieve her burden.

"You said an hour. Did anyone give you trouble?" He had to resist the urge to run his hands over her to check for any marks or injuries. She smiled exhaustedly and shook her head.

"Nothing I couldn't handle." As he took another bag from her hand, he noticed rusty smears across her knuckles. He grabbed the hand and gave her a concerned look. She just smiled again. "Like I said. Handled."

Eddies of conflicting emotions churned through him—anger at whoever threatened her, relief that she was okay, pride that she was able to hold her own even down here. Without thinking, he said in a low voice, "Good girl."

Sonia snatched her hand back, suddenly short of breath and pointedly avoiding eye contact. "Oh, boy. Umm, let's just get this unpacked."

Once they dumped out all the bags, Haez could see just how extensive Sonia's idea of a disguise could be. Other than the makeup and clothing, he didn't even know what half the items were.

"Did you at least save enough money for the casino?" he asked, examining a package of greyish putty. She snatched it out of his hand and dragged a chair over to sit by the bed.

"You'll have money to do your job," she said, pointing towards the chair. "Now sit down and let me do mine."

8

Sonia

Sonia stood in front of Haez as he sat in the lounge chair and she focused on patting yellow-orange pancake makeup over his face. Her mind kept wandering back to him holding her hand, and his words.

Good girl.

Another shiver went through her. The filthy talk the night before may have gotten Sonia worked up, but the sound of him saying those two little words drilled into her brain and sent shivers down her spine. Thankfully he kept his eyes closed as she worked, letting her examine him more closely.

He really was handsome, in a mephite way. All his features were sharp—jutting cheekbones, pointed chin, ears rising to knife-sharp points. Even his gaunt, sunken cheeks just emphasized the shape of his face. His body added to the effect. He wasn't obviously muscled like her but was far from feeble. All his strength was lean and sleek, like a sinuous snake that could break bones with its crushing squeeze.

And tall. Don't forget tall. Part of her lamented having to disguise him so much. It felt like using crayon to cover up an oil painting. The modeling putty she had applied to his face changed his features subtly enough to trick a roving eye, and dental adhesive secured a chip of plaster in the gap of his missing tooth. But the lighter colour would be doing most of the heavy lifting for disguising him—that and the gaudy gold horn caps, which were the sort of tacky mephite adornment only indulged by young crooks getting their first taste of money. At least according to the irritable shop girl who'd sold them to her.

While she would insist it was purely practical for balancing out his horns, it did make her giggle to think how foolish he would look to other mephites. It was a shame he wouldn't take character-building seriously; she could get so much good material out of such a little accessory.

Once she finished blending the makeup down his neck, she spritzed him with a setting spray.

"Keep your eyes shut while that dries," she said. He nodded his acknowledgement while Sonia reached to his hands, patting more colour on. She pushed up his sleeve to cover his wrists and found a thin golden bracelet clinging to the skin of his forearm.

She tugged at it lightly with one finger. "Can you take this off?"

Without opening his eyes, Haez gave a small, amused huff. "Really?"

"Yeah? Why? What is it?" Sonia ran her fingers around the bracelet. Upon closer inspection, she realized it didn't have any visible latch and was much stronger than such a delicate loop should be.

"A token to mark those indentured to the Sabres. Only Staukar and his inner circle know how to remove them. Mostly meant to be a deterrent for transports that might help a contracted worker leave the planet before their debts are paid. No one wants to risk getting on their bad side. You've never wondered why you have to show your wrists at the spaceport?"

Sonia hadn't been to a spaceport since she'd arrived on Quantrin. There wasn't any family left for her to go to and never enough money to justify traveling for pleasure. She didn't say it, though, instead shrugging and replying, "I guess I never thought about it that much."

She went silent, fingering the thin chain that now looked as heavy as an ebion shackle. Haez's opposite hand moved to cover hers, giving a gentle squeeze.

"It's alright," he said quietly. "For what it's worth, I'm glad you didn't have to know."

Sonia's heart stuttered at the feel of his warm hand on hers and his soft, sad voice.

Oh, Haez.

She took a steadying breath and tried to keep her voice light. "Well, it's not a problem. I can secure it higher as long as you can keep your sleeves down."

He nodded and released her hand. It didn't take much longer for her to smear adhesive on his forearm to hold back the bracelet and finish turning his hands yellow. When she finished, she used the setting spray on his hands and pulled back.

"Wave your hands," she said, shaking her own even as his eyes stayed closed. He followed her directions, drying out the spray while she moved back to the bed and laid out their respective outfits. All-black for both—they needed to look nice, not flashy.

"Alright, clothes are on the bed. Be careful not to smudge the makeup while you're getting dressed. I'll get ready in the washroom."

"Do you need any help?"

She looked back to meet his gaze, eyes coppery and just as striking as the rest of him.

Good girl.

"Nope," she squeaked, "nope, nope, nope."

Sonia scurried to the washroom with her dress and hoped that she wouldn't be forced to learn more about herself today. Otherwise, she was liable to die of a heart attack before they even made it off planet.

· · · · ● · ● · · · ·

Once she was alone, she threw herself into the meditative process of making her character. Today she needed to be arm candy, prepared to drape herself on anyone with money and loose lips. Every slimeball's lucky charm. She practiced her facial expressions while contouring—lascivious, but non-threatening; mysterious, but not so much that you cared to learn her story. Most importantly, willing to do anything for enough money. Once she finished, a new personality faced her in the mirror.

Waundi, she decided.

She slicked her hair back from her face in a way that she hoped would disguise the hack-job cut as elegant. Lastly, the dress. The neckline plunged so deep that it nearly ran into the hip-high slit cut up the side. Restrictive, uncomfortable, and one false move away from public indecency. Sonia would never wear it, but Waundi would.

Leaving the washroom, she saw Haez fiddling with the final fastenings of his outfit. As she expected, it was a perfect fit and emphasized the lines of his body perfectly, with its high collar and sleek, slim-cut trousers. In a different life, she could have been a stylist. The thought filled her with smug satisfaction.

He looked up at the sound of the washroom door sliding open and paused, gaping at her. After a thick swallow, he forced out, "You look nice."

Sonia giggled indulgently and leaned into his body. "I'm glad you like it. You deserve to feel lucky today."

Haez's face closed off and went cold. "Don't do that. It's just us."

Sonia gritted her teeth in a smile. "We talked about this, baby. Don't be mean."

He stared at her for a moment before shoving his arm out for her to grab. She did so graciously, but as they left their room, she wished she could have stayed Sonia for a little while longer. The job took priority, though, and that required commitment to the bit. She clung to his lean arm and cast him a sideways glance as he hailed them a glider.

Good girl.

•••••●•●••••

When the glider slowed in front of the casino, Sonia blinked against the obtrusive, glittering lights that covered the section of tower. Who needed the sun from above when this monstrosity shone nearly as bright? The casino occupied the entire height of the skyscraper for the level, stretching as high as a full residential block before abruptly changing to another gambling den's colours at the next level's spread of walkways. Nearly every other tower mirrored it, either through the glitter of casinos, the lurid red glow of the brothels, or the decadent restaurants and shops that latched onto the foot traffic drawn in by the real attractions.

The glider lane deposited them at an upper entrance, the doors folding downwards to form a ramp bridging the gap between the vehicle and the platform. Haez slid across the wide bench seats and exited first, reaching back to steady Sonia on her delicate heels as she crossed the space. She gave a polite nod to the doorman as they entered while Haez tried to look casual rubbing at his neck.

"This makeup is itching the shit out of me," he muttered.

"Don't you dare rub it off," she said sweetly through her teeth, her smile unfaltering. "Hands on me, handsome."

She pulled the hand away from his neck and guided it to rest on her waist. He gripped her close as they stepped in onto the grand entryway, which formed a balcony overlooking the main casino floor.

Sonia had never seen such an opulent space. It seemed like every inch was covered in gold and velvet, even the plush carpet underfoot feeling too rich for her peasant's feet to touch. It was topped off by a massive chandelier that hung close to eye-level on the balcony and cast dabbles of sparkling light over the patrons and tables below.

She should have been basking in the glamour that she had only ever witnessed in her grandmother's old holodramas. But her eyes couldn't stop looking at the wrists of the employees—the doorman, the bar tender, the human girl being groped by a drunk mephite as they waited for a lift to the attached hotel rooms. All had the same thin gold bracelets as Haez. It made the glamour feel like ash in her mouth.

Her character faltered as they looked out over the floor and all its trapped workers. "Is everyone here indentured?" she asked, voice laced with disgust.

"Not everyone," Haez muttered bitterly. "Most, though. People get given jobs based on their skills. Some run drugs like me. But a lot of gamblers never leave the casino."

Sonia gaped in shock at the sheer volume of workers. "This can't all be from gamblers."

"No. There's lots of ways to end up in hock to Staukar. I think the brothels are mostly users. If you cut someone off from their supply, it doesn't take long for them to sign away their life if it'll guarantee a fix."

As Haez said the words, a lift door slid open off to the side. A wiloh woman stepped out, adjusting her dress and tidying the fleshy tendrils that hung like hair from her scalp, golden bracelet swaying on her wrist. Her face was flat and emotionless as she checked herself in a compact mirror. Once she fixed the lipstick smudged across her florescent-blue chin, she snapped the mirror shut and took on a casually seductive expression before descending the stairs that led to the main gambling floor. Seeing someone else doing it, she understood why it made Haez shudder.

So, this was the real Quantrin. This was what Ottok had been protecting her against. He was right—she hadn't realized just how trapped in the life a person could be. Suddenly, it felt like none of it mattered. Not her tourist scams, not her characters, not her stupid fucking makeup. She wanted the city to collapse on itself. She wanted Staukar to burn.

Haez turned and leaned against the banister, peering at Sonia's face. "Who are you?"

Sonia gave him a confused look and asked, "What?"

His face quirked into a charming smile, and he asked again, "Who are *you*?" putting a flirtatious emphasis on the last word.

Oh, right. He was trying to help her get the character back. She gave a small chuckle and took a deep breath, letting her posture relax and her hip sway out to the side. When she exhaled and opened her eyes, it was with a sly smile.

"I'm Waundi, honey. You looking for a lucky charm?"

He grabbed and kissed the back of her hand, "Yes, I am, Waundi." He took her around the waist again and led her towards the stairs. As they descended, he murmured in her ear.

"Welcome to *The Celeste.*"

9

Sonia

The pair stepped onto the main casino floor and into the cacophony of colour, noise, and people. All around them were patrons in their evening best clamouring at the thrind tables, groaning and complaining over an oppos game, or mindlessly pulling the levers of jangling slot machines.

Sonia scanned the cavernous space, smiling slyly at every man they passed. She had to start courting targets early so she would be on their mind when it was time for her to work. Through the smile, she leaned into Haez, asking, "Can you spot anything promising?"

"Don't need to. I know where we need to be." He nodded his chin towards a back corner, which was blocked off from the clamour by low walls and ringed with guards. "That's the high-rollers' table. Usually for VIPs, but there's a handful of Staukar's favourite hustlers who stay there. They'll pull anyone from the floor who's on a hot streak to knock them down a peg." His face turned grim. "That's how I started owing Staukar money. They'll bleed you dry and then send you to ask for a loan. Once that's gone, you get offered a contract."

As if on cue, a gallan with a fraction as many beak-piercings as Ottok stood from the table and staggered away looking shellshocked. He smoothed down his feathers and moved towards the stairs that led up to an office overlooking the floor. Her heart clenched thinking of a younger and more naïve Haez leaving that table with the same face of despair and the same defeated posture as he marched to sign away his future.

Looking up at the frosted flexiglass that enclosed the upper office, Sonia tensed when she saw a silhouette standing and moving to meet the newest victim.

"He's not up there, right?"

"Staukar? Not likely. He's got more important things to think about than minding the money."

Sonia let out her held breath, but another concern wriggled into her thoughts. She swung in front of him and walked backwards while holding his hands. The flirtatious smile never dropped even as her eyes bored into his. "How can you be sure they aren't just going to fleece you again?"

"They like to play with their food. They'll drive the pot up and let you win for a while, then once you're cocky enough to bet away your soul, they'll snatch it back. The trick is to stop while you're ahead."

"And *can* you?" Sonia asked, the worry in her eyes evident even through the mask of Waundi.

Haez opened his mouth in mock-offense and put his hand over his heart. "Does my lucky charm doubt me?"

"Please just tell me you're not going to lose all our money."

Haez smiled and leaned down, his jutting yellow nose grazing along side her own. "I'm not going to lose all our money."

She threw her head back, laughing like he'd just told her the funniest joke she could imagine. Inside, she pretended that the flip-flopping in her stomach was just anxiety.

Swinging back to his side, she said, "Pick your table, hotshot. Somewhere in the middle. I need to be visible."

His hand tightened slightly on her waist. When he spoke, there was audible tension in his voice. "I don't know. It might attract guards if we're too obvious."

Sonia was confused and tried to keep the same light voice as she said, "Too obvious? Haez, look at how many women are here. Obvious is the only way I'll get noticed."

Haez looked around the room like he only just realized there were other women there at all. Still, he pursed his lips and stayed petulantly silent. Sonia gave him a concerned look.

"This was the plan, baby. What's gotten into you?"

"Nothing," he replied tersely, guiding her towards an oppos table in the centre of the floor. It was crowded with participants and observers, and as one frustrated player threw down his cards to leave, Haez slid into the open seat, tugging Sonia down to sit across his lap. She leaned back into his arm and crossed her legs to let a tawny thigh slide out of the dress' slit as he was dealt in. There were lots of other women around the table, putting on similar performances. She cast an eye at the other players to see which ones seemed interested in her over the others, and who among them might know something about clandestine transports. It left her with a handful of targets to make eyes at once Haez moved to the big table.

It may have just been vanity, but Sonia also snuck a look at Haez through her eyelashes, wondering if he was being drawn to anyone else around the table. After all, she wasn't the kind of breakable human she'd been led to believe he preferred. It gave her a confusing sense of pleasure seeing that he seemed uninterested in anything at the table other than the cards he was dealt and the handful of her thigh that he was gripping and massaging absently. Not that it mattered. Not that she cared. Because she didn't.

It was still nice though.

When he started hyper focusing on the game, it at least confirmed her assumptions about his ability to work a card table. The first hand he won with ease, drawing a few irritated glares from the other players. Haez gave another squeeze to the thigh he'd been palming.

"Looks like you are lucky, sweetness," he said, giving a wink to his opponents. Sonia nuzzled his neck and ground herself down into his groin. He gave a dark growl in his throat and swatted her backside, nearly as exposed as her leg as the dress rode up farther. With a giggle, she tossed her head back and stole another glance at the rest of the table to see who of her original targets was being pulled in by her display.

Nothing. Every one that had been salivating over her now hid their faces behind hands of coffin-shaped cards. These low-lives would have to be made of stone for none of them to be interested, so what . . .

Sonia looked to Haez and bristled with annoyance. He glared down at the other players murderously, hand even tighter around her waist. So much for letting her do her job.

"What are you doing?" she bit out through a strained smile. When he didn't reply, she leaned into his pointed ear like she was whispering him a filthy promise. "I don't know what the fuck is going on with you, but you need to get your shit together. If you keep this up, no one will dare talk to me after you go. If no one talks to me, I can't find us a transport."

After a moment, he took a deep, steadying breath. He turned and put his forehead against hers, his horn caps pushing indentations into her hair. "I don't like it," he said quietly, like they were now engrossed in private dirty talk. "These guys are losers. They won't have any info."

"That's not your call, baby. Can you let me do my job?"

He flicked his copper eyes to hers and pinned her with his stare. "Don't let any of them touch you."

She briefly considered getting up to drape herself over one of his opponents. That would show him for trying to tell her what to do. But his eyes bored into her like a tether, and she liked the anchoring feeling.

"I'll try."

Haez eased his grip on her waist and nuzzled his forehead against hers a last time. With a renewed smile, he turned his attention back to the table.

"Sorry, fellas, where were we?"

· · · · · ● · ● · · · ·

It took time for Haez work the table, the pile of credits in front of him growing as players joined and eventually cycled back out, creditless and scowling. Watching how easily he was able to win hand after hand made Sonia deeply anxious about what he would be encountering at the next table—after all, even if Haez had only been half as good in his youth as he was now, it would still have been frightening to bet against the kind of people who could deal such a devastating loss to such a skilled player.

But they had a plan, and if Haez was trusting Sonia to do her job, she had to trust him too. And she played her part well—rubbing his shoulders, nibbling his ear, showing off her body enough that any onlookers would be hungry for a taste of whatever he was having. At the same time, she kept a subtle eye on the employees, and when she saw the dealer gesture toward the guards for the high-stakes game, she bent down to mutter in his ear, "They're on the hook."

Haez reached back and brushed a knuckle along her jaw in acknowledgement before revealing yet another winning hand. Groans went up around the table again and the dealer, looking increasingly fed-up with his antics, pushed another pile of wagers towards Haez. He made a show of stretching his back and standing.

"I think that's it for me. Gonna quit while I'm ahead," he said as he gathered his winnings. When they turned to walk from the table, their path was blocked by a pair of guards.

"You've been requested to join a private game," one of them stated flatly. Haez played it up, preening at the invitation.

"Nice to see that someone recognizes talent. Lead the way," he said to the guard. He turned back to Sonia and said, "Sorry, sweetness. This won't be any place for a lady. Wait for me at the bar?"

"Don't be too long," she pouted. "You know I get bored easy."

He kissed her hand before being led away to the private table. *Don't lose all our money*, she willed at his retreating back. There wasn't anything else she could do as she watched him be seated and disappear behind the broad-shouldered guards blocking the entrance. With a sigh, she moved to the bar, slid into an empty stool, and crossed her legs again, letting the bait out to await bites.

Sonia prided herself on being able to read people. As much as she disliked the tourist scam, one of her favourite ways to do it was to go to a random bar and challenge herself to identify a target as fast as possible and see how much she could glean. And appearances told much.

As men began to filter over to try their luck flirting with the lonely human, she watched them in the mirrored backsplash behind the bar and assessed them on approach. Dressed too ostentatiously? Probably tourists themselves. A straight, even stride? Too law-abiding—anyone who regularly carried a weapon developed a lean to compensate for the weight. Obviously a rough-and-tumble criminal? Definitely a cop. This didn't even consider those who would have fit what she was looking for if not for the waxy quality of their skin and the green-ringed splotches that marred their hands and arms. She knew from her parents what those indicated. Even as means to an end, she refused to work with anyone with those particular vices.

Before they could say their first pickup lines, she already knew if they were the right fit for her needs and she gently moved them along one after another. A comment about waiting for her boyfriend and a nod towards the VIP area was enough to deter all unsuitable candidates.

She was starting to worry that the plan would be a bust when another figure came into view, glancing from side to side on his approach and trying to look less obviously interested than he was. A yreet, small for his people but huge for everyone else. Not tall and sleek like Haez. Yreets were four-armed walls of meat, with everything from their heavy, bulging shoulders to their stretched, beige faces denoting width and strength.

This one was wearing nice clothes to be sure, possibly nicer than many of the other patrons. But they were stiff, and he squirmed against the restrictive lines. Brand-new clothes in a style to which he was unaccustomed. Then there were his hands—scrubbed clean but still stained black at the fingertips. Engine grease. Finally, the subtle red bloom and dry skin on his face, which happened over time with constant exposure to the ambient radiation of hyperspace through a viewscreen.

Before he slid into the seat next to her, she knew he was a spacer. And if he was in an establishment like this, he was the exact kind of law-agnostic person they needed. Perfect.

Sonia sipped her cocktail as he grunted and sat on the little stool, which creaked under his bulk. She pretended not to have noticed him, letting him order his own drink as she mulled over her angle.

Considering how much he had splashed out, he may have recently taken command of his own starship. He'd be feeling powerful and bold. If he thought there were the promise of a pretty human girl-friend, he might feel bold enough to smuggle out a tragically trapped woman like herself. *Make him feel like a hero. Creeps love that,* she thought. It would be difficult to get him to take Haez voluntarily, especially if he was seen as a threat to the captain's claim. But that's what the cart was for. He could hide out and they would be halfway to the next sector before it became a problem. Easy.

Angle in mind, she tried to look a little distant and sad, absently running a finger around the edge of her glass. It took a few minutes of him drinking and working up courage before he finally grunted, "I haven't seen you here before."

Like she only just noticed he was there, she swung her gaze to him. After a moment, she gave a light laugh and little smile.

"I suppose I am new. It feels like I've been here for years. You looking for a little luck, honey?"

He gave a proud smirk. "I've had some pretty good luck already. But I wouldn't say no to a little more."

As he leaned in and set one of his hands on her bare thigh, an uneasy feeling crept up her spine. Like she was being watched.

She looked towards the high rollers' table. Between the guards, she could see Haez's eyes burning out, staring daggers at her target. Sonia met his stare, pointedly took the yreet's hand in her own and moved it off her leg. Haez's face softened but his eyes stayed pinned on them. *Focus, Sonia. Vulnerable. Sexy and vulnerable.*

"I'm not sure how lucky I am right now. I'm here, after all."

"It's not all that bad here, is it?" Another of his four hands crept up to caress her back. Sonia willed Haez to focus on his game and just let her work.

"You're a spacer, aren't you? I can always tell. What's it like, getting to ride through the stars every day?" She filled her voice with wonderment. The yreet's wide mouth split into a grey-toothed smile. The hand landed on her back and one of his thick fingers slid under the fabric of her dress.

"You got a good eye. You wanting a *ride* through the stars, beautiful?" His stare turned lascivious with the emphasis.

The optimism Sonia had been feeling popped like a bubble. What a waste of her fucking time. The guy wasn't going to do anything altruistically. At most, he would try to get her into bed and string her along with promises of escape that would never pay off. She didn't want to contemplate his worst.

No matter. They had plenty of time and she couldn't let one misread target throw her off her character. Maybe it was time to get back to the tables to find the targets that felt too noble to make the first move. Haez would just have to cope with not being able to spy on her.

She gave him another smile and stood from her stool. "You make a tempting offer, honey. Maybe next time—I'm back on the clock."

She tried blowing him a kiss and turning to leave, but one of the yreet's huge hands clamped over her wrist like a vise. She gave a nervous laugh and said, "Come on, honey. You don't want me getting in trouble, do you?"

Something menacing crept into his face. "What's your job?"

"What?"

"I know what they keep human girls for here. You're back on the clock. So where do you think you're going?"

Stupid, stupid, stupid. Why did she say she was working? She gave another giggle to try to simmer him down. "I'm a waitress, silly. I'm not—"

"You think I'm stupid? A stupid spacer who's not worth your time?" He stood from the stool and started to drag her away from the bar. Sonia tried to dig in and pull her arm back, but her delicate heels skidded against the polished floor.

"Hey! Get—"

"I got a room upstairs. You shut your whore mouth and do your job, or I'll let your boss know I didn't feel so welcomed."

A thrill of fear went through her. Usually when she pulled this grift, it was on law-abiding levels. If things went sideways, a scream for help was all it took to defuse things long enough to get away. Not to mention that she wasn't usually pulling it in a venue owned by someone who would rather her be dead. Who knew how much worse things could get if she did cry for help.

Stupid, stupid little girl. She threw a panicked look back to Haez's table.

Gone. Seat empty and half his winnings abandoned on the table. Everything felt still and quiet and alone. She was alone again.

Suddenly she was too shellshocked to fight against the drag on her arm. Her eyes drifted down to her own feet as she stumbled forward in defeat. She was broken out of it when the yreet stopped and yelled at someone, "Move it, moron. I got a date."

Sonia looked up and saw Haez. But something was wrong. She may have only met him a few days ago, but she knew his face and his expressions well—even through the yellow makeup. She knew what he looked like angry. The man she saw now looked like bloodlust given form.

His expression was flat except for his furious copper eyes bugging out of his head and the slightest hint of an angry red flush creeping through the makeup. At the yreet's yell, his mouth took on a horrible smile that showed every tooth in his head.

Haez grabbed the yreet's face in both hands and slammed it down against a card table with a sick crunch. The players shrieked and scattered when a splatter of blood sprayed across their cards. Then he did it again.

And again.

And again.

Sonia was frozen, watching her only ally bash another person's head into a bloody clump. There was no way he should have been that strong, even with the extra height he had on the yreet. When she got breath back in her lungs, she croaked, "Haez?"

Somehow, her quiet voice cut through whatever red mist had consumed Haez. His head whipped around to look at her and she took a step back, a new spark of fear blooming at the sight of his blood-splattered face. Looking at Sonia, his eyes softened. Then he looked back at the yreet, still alive but barely twitching on the floor.

"Why did you do that?" she whispered pleadingly. He gave her a look full of confusion and distress.

"I don't know."

From behind them came the whir of plasma guns preparing shots. Four guards in face-covering helmets stood in a line with their guns trained on Haez. He slowly turned to face them, rubbing some of the blood away from his eye before raising his hands. Sonia cursed him silently. That absent-minded action had rubbed the slightest bit of yellow off his skin, allowing a shadow of burgundy to peek through the putty.

She prayed they would assume it was just a bruise or that the remaining blood would distract. One of the guards looked to her and asked, "Do you know this man, miss?"

Before she could respond, Haez spat, "No." Sonia looked at him and he gave a tiny shake of his head. She turned back to the guards.

"That's right. Never met him in my life."

A tall mephite guard stepped forward and spoke back at the rest. "I'll take this one to lockup. We'll see what the boss wants done with him." Turning to Sonia, he added, "You should follow along, miss. I'll have to take your witness statement afterwards."

The other guards nodded and dispersed to monitor the floor. The remaining guard unhooked binders from his belt and secured Haez's hands behind his back. He then jerked his gun to get Haez to walk towards a set of double-doors. Sonia fell in step behind and started frantically going over possibilities. Bashing the guard in the head when they were out of sight of the main room? The helmet was a problem. She considered faking fainting so Haez could get the jump on him, but screamed internally, *this isn't a damn holodrama, Sonia! Think better!*

The doors slid open and led them into a back hallway. When they swished shut behind them, the guard stopped and looked up and down the hall. With a sigh, he reached up to his helmet.

"Makeup, Haez? Really?" he asked, unclipping the front of the helmet and revealing the blue face of another mephite man. Haez's face turned furious and he struggled against the binders.

"Proll, you gloxig-fucking bastard!" he yelled. When the binders wouldn't budge, he put his head down to try charging him with his horns. Proll reached out and lazily shoved the top of his bent head, putting him off-balance and tumbling back onto his ass. The horn caps fell off and went clattering across the floor. Sonia rushed to his side, looking furiously up at the guard.

"You're the one who gave him the bad job."

"No," he sighed, easing the back shell of the helmet off over his horns. "No, that was my brother. Haez, what in the hells were you thinking coming here? Do you have a death wish?"

"What do you care?" he snarled back at Proll. "Just call your boss and get it over with. Maybe he'll let you kiss his little prick."

"I had nothing to do with that! Rakir didn't tell me what he was doing. I wouldn't have let him if he had." At Haez's scoffing, Proll continued, "I'm serious. Rakir, he . . . he doesn't always think things through. He was trying to get ahead with Staukar, and this was the half-baked plan he landed on. You were just convenient."

Haez scowled up at him. Sonia set a soothing hand on his shoulder and spoke to Proll. "Where is he now?"

"With Staukar. He's been insisting that Rakir be with him to co-ordinate searches." An uneasy shiver went through Proll's shoulders. "It's bad, Haez. My brother can handle some serious shit, but even he's nervous around Staukar now. I think he's cracked. You need to get off Quantrin."

"And where were you?" Haez cut in. "When you should have been babysitting your psycho twin? Where were you?"

Proll's face flushed purple. "I had . . . private matters." Haez stared at him until Proll grimaced and added, "Come on, man. There's a lady present."

Haez's mouth opened with understanding and then twisted with disgust. Sonia looked between the two of them. "What? What is it?"

"Nothing," the men said in unison. She shook her head and walked to retrieve Haez's horn caps.

"We're *trying* to get off Quantrin," Haez said to Proll. "That's why we came here. Do you know anyone who could move us? Someone who wouldn't look too closely at the luggage?"

Proll stared at Haez blankly for a moment before giving a scoff and shaking his head. "No. I'm a casino guard, not an information broker. And I sure hope you grabbed some of your money before that outburst, 'cause you sure as shit aren't getting it back now. Pretty rich, calling Rakir a psycho, all things considered."

Haez gave him a sour look and turned back to Sonia. "Did you have any luck?"

Sonia shook her head as she came back and started replacing the caps. "I only spoke with the one guy. I can go back and try again." Even as she said it, her skin crawled, remembering the iron grip on her wrist.

"No," Haez blurts, avoiding eye contact. Sonia narrowed her eyes at him.

"I'm not the one who blew up our chances of getting information here."

"Did you want me to just sit there and watch while—"

"I don't know, Haez!" Sonia shouted. "I don't think the solution was to turn his skull into a piñata!"

"I don't know what is!"

As they bickered back and forth, Proll put a finger to his ear, listening to some radio chatter. "Shhh," he said. They both went silent and watched him as he listened.

"Where were you holed up?" Proll asked.

"A motel a few towers away from here," Haez said cautiously, "Why?"

"Did anyone see you? A litto?"

Sonia and Haez shared a panicked look. "A litto checked us in," Sonia said to Proll. He nodded and moved to remove Haez's binders.

"It just turned up. Apparently, it'll only talk to Staukar and he'll need time to get down from the upper levels. Maybe a couple hours. There's an emergency exit at the end of this hall. Cross over to the next tower before you try to hail a glider."

Haez stood and dusted himself off. His face was pinched-looking as he forced out a, "Thank you."

Proll gave a weak smile and said, "Will you do me a favour? Don't judge Rakir too badly for this. It was a fucked-up thing to do but he had his reasons."

Haez's brows shot up as he gave Proll an incredulous look. He looked back at Sonia in disbelief before turning back to Proll with a finger raised.

"Both of us," he started, using the finger to gesture between him and Sonia, "are on the run because of your brother. And you want us to spare kind thoughts for him? Because he wanted to be promoted to killer-in-chief?"

Proll's face was stony and distant when he replied, "I *am* sorry, Haez. I really am. I hope you get off this planet and never have to come back. But a lot of us don't have that option. And we do what we must to survive. We become what we have to."

Sonia felt a rush of sympathy for Proll, with his graceful hands that looked like they were never meant to hold a gun and wan skin that never had a chance to be enriched by the warmth of real sunsets. His eyes flicked to Sonia and she nodded. Haez might never truly understand, but she did. She reached for Haez's hand and squeezed it in her own.

"We need to go."

He returned her grasp, and with one last look to Proll, they took off running for the exit. There wasn't much time. Sonia willed for a fast glider to pick them up.

10

Haez

When their glider swooped into the lot outside the motel, they were past keeping any pretense of calm. Instead, they both flew into motion, sprinting down the glider ramp and into their room. Haez started throwing any trace of their stay into the cart, treasures and empty food wrappers alike. Sonia yanked off her delicate heels, tossed them in the cart, and jammed her feet back into her flat climbing shoes before cleaning up behind Haez. They didn't need to say it out loud to know their best chance was in making the litto look like a liar to buy some time. Hopefully, it would make others who may have seen them think twice about trying for their own paydays.

Haez shoved their still-damp towels into the cart as Sonia finished tucking the sheets in tidy hospital corners around the mattress. Sweat was digging burgundy trails into Haez's yellow makeup.

"How are we doing?" Haez asked.

Sonia jerked her head toward the immaculate room, surfaces far cleaner and bed much neater than when they'd arrived. "They'd have to swab to be sure it was us. The missing towels are going to look weird, but its better than leaving them wet."

Haez nodded and ripped off his own dress shoes, replacing them with his boots. "We can go over the platform edge. Keep going down." He saw her shudder and continued, "Just for now. We need room to breathe."

"I'm not arguing," she muttered. She pulled the skirt of her dress back at the slit and knotted it up on her opposite hip, letting her legs move freely. As Haez pushed the cart towards the door, she moved to the panel beside the frame.

"Ready?" she asked. At Haez's nod, she hit the panel to slide the door open.

Haez pushed the cart at a harsh jog, trying to shove it faster than its protesting motor would allow. Sonia ran out after him and sprinted past. She snatched up towels, makeup, anything that could be spared to make room, and ran to the platform edge. The armful of objects was hurled over the railing, sending them fluttering and clanging into the depths.

When Haez reached the railing, he moved his hands underneath to give it a boost over. "C'mon, c'mon," he muttered to Sonia. She grabbed under the opposite side and helped it to hover up and over. It floated out over the abyss, when they heard an unmistakable sound.

Approaching gliders. A whole fleet of them from the volume.

"A couple hours, my ass," Haez growled, practically throwing Sonia onto the cart in his haste to help her. She landed with a *flump* and wasted no time securing herself. Haez smacked the side controls to start the cart's descent before climbing the railing. It was below him when he dropped over and landed flat on his back. The whirring sound grew louder and the yellow artificial lights dotting the side of a nearby skyscraper were distorted by the approaching vehicles.

"We're too exposed. They're going to see us," Sonia whispered, eyes wide with panic. Haez hit the controls again to stop their descent. Before she could hiss at him to get it moving, he pressed another button to send them gliding sideways. He nestled them under the grated floor of the lot and stopped underneath a pair of parked gliders. It was a trick he had picked up while smuggling between levels—if you were desperate enough to cling to the bottom of a walkway with nothing separating you from a lethal fall, you could hide from just about anyone, law enforcement and gangsters alike. They were invisible to the convoy of mismatched gliders now converging on the motel above them, formed of any members who happened to be close by. Through the grate, however, they could still peer out towards their abandoned room.

A pair of luxury gliders swooped in and stopped before being flanked by utilitarian bricks. The door of one of the plain gliders folded down and the litto scuttled down the ramp on the fingertips of its lower hands while its upper ones twisted together anxiously. More ramps folded down, and from within streamed a dozen Sabre enforcers; an array of plainly clothed men whose cold eyes and quietly pleased smiles revealed their excitement for the cruelty to come. Once they took their positions on either side of the door to their abandoned room, Vrix emerged from one of the nice gliders, followed by Rakir with his face in its usual emotionless mask. After they scanned the lot, Vrix tapped one of his fists twice against the last glider. Finally, Staukar descended alone, clearly not deigning to share his vehicle with anyone but his chauffeur. The litto rushed forward and scurried beside Staukar. Haez could hear its excitable jabbering drifting down through the grating.

"You're not going to regret this, Mr. Staukar, sir. I keep an eye on things, right? I know everyone who comes through here. A small fee and I'll tell you anything you need to know. This tip is on the house, of course. Y'know, because we're friends now."

Staukar remained silent, though Haez recognized the irritated tension through his shoulders. It may have sold them out, but he still found himself willing the litto to just shut up for its own sake. Standing outside the door, Staukar said curtly, "Open it."

The litto sputtered to a stop and nodded. It tapped its keycard against the sensor and the door slid open. The proud expression on its face dropped when it saw the clean and empty room. Staukar cooly turned his attention to the litto.

"And this was the room he was in?" he said. The litto nodded frantically, looking from Staukar to the room like maybe the occupants were hiding just around the corner.

"I swear, sir, he was here! A mephite with a fucked horn, right? He had some human girl with him too!" Haez silently cursed—any chance that Sonia could've had of vanishing off into some isolated neighbourhood on the far side of Quantrin was fucked now. She was good, but not perfect. At least one camera would have spotted her that night—with enough techs on the case, it would be a few days at most before she was identified.

The litto's hands were gesticulating wildly as it kept jabbering. "They were supposed to stay for a week. It was him; I know it was him!" Its panicked face brightened, and it reached one of its lower hands into a pocket, producing the bracelet that Haez had given it as payment. "See? He gave me this to pay for the room. It was him!"

Staukar took the bracelet from the litto and let it drape over his hand as he examined it. An icy feeling flooded Haez's gut when Staukar smiled. Turning towards Vrix and Rakir, he said, "This was a gift from my father. Their thirtieth anniversary, I believe. Beautiful, isn't it?"

"Very beautiful, sir," Vrix replied flatly while Rakir only gave a silent nod. Staukar's mild smile didn't drop as he turned back to the litto.

"How long was it you said they were staying?"

"A week, Mr. Staukar. They should still—"

"So, he provided you with my late father's thirtieth anniversary gift to my mother," Staukar interrupted, tucking the bracelet into his breast pocket, "and you valued it as a one-week stay at this motel?"

Oh no.

Haez whispered to Sonia, "Don't look." Sonia looked at him, then carefully turned in the cart to not make noise. Even with her back to the scene, she scrunched her eyes shut. Haez watched. Someone had to bear witness—its family deserved that much.

The litto realized its mistake too late and stammered, "No, but he—"

In one smooth action, Staukar unholstered his gun and fired a bolt through one of the litto's lower segments. It screamed and writhed, its whole body dropping against the grating in its agony. Through its gasping and blubbering, it tried again, "Please sir, I didn't—"

Staukar fired another shot through the end of its body, the vicious glee now plain on his face. Rakir didn't flinch, his face betraying nothing, but his knuckles were white where they clenched around his own wrist in front of his body, and he stared at a spot on the tower wall instead of at the shrieking litto.

"I'm sorry!" it screamed out, clasping its upper hands together in a plea. "I'm sorry. Please!"

Staukar's mouth popped open in a silent 'oh' and he holstered his gun. "An apology. That's all I wanted." He turned his attention to the enforcers. "What are you all standing around for? The poor creature's tail is injured." He moved to reboard his glider and spoke over his shoulder.

"Remove it."

The men descended on the litto. Staukar disappeared into his glider after muttering something to Vrix and Rakir, who nodded and looked on as the bruisers took to the screaming litto with bludgeons and blades. Haez had to avert his eyes to not be sick and saw that Sonia had her hands pressed over her ears. When he heard the first ripping crunch of a segment separating, he almost did the same. But then there was the sizzling zing of a laser bolt and the litto went silent.

He looked back in surprise. Staukar's glider was nowhere to be seen. The litto lay still on the ground with a smoking hole in its head as Rakir holstered his gun. The confused men looked from the body to Vrix, who was giving Rakir a stern stare. Rakir shrugged and said, "They removed it."

Vrix held the stare a moment longer before yelling, "We're wasting time. They're bartering the jewellery. Hit every pawn shop on this level. See who knows where they're going." He waved a hand vaguely at a pair of enforcers. "You two toss the worm."

When Vrix spoke, the men snapped to attention and obeyed with militant discipline. The pair disposing of the litto passed dangerously close to Haez and Sonia's hiding spot but were too focused on their task to notice them. The pieces went sailing past and Haez gave silent thanks that Sonia's eyes were still squeezed shut. All the underlings returned to their gliders and took off, leaving behind only Vrix and Rakir. Rakir moved to reboard their glider, but Vrix stopped him with one of his huge hands on his elbow.

"You know full-well what he meant, Rakir," Vrix said. Rakir's jaw clenched and he stubbornly avoided eye contact.

"It was unnecessary," he replied.

"No shit. But you're not doing hits anymore. You're working with the boss, and you don't want to get on his bad side. If he makes it clear that he wants things taken slow, just do it. You got your brother to think about."

Rakir jerked his arm away from Vrix and stormed back up the ramp. Vrix gave a frustrated sigh before following him in and moments later, the ramp folded up and the glider took off across the level.

Haez let out a held breath and touched Sonia's arm. She opened her eyes and gave him a questioning look. He nodded, and she removed her hands from her ears. Haez pressed the controls to start descending, hoping against hope they didn't have to see where the litto landed.

• • • • ● • ● • • • •

It wasn't until the platform vanished from sight completely that they breathed easy again. Sonia passed out from exhaustion, curled in a little ball on her side of the cart, her hair in disarray. Haez stayed alert and watched her, one hand hovering slightly in case she woke suddenly and panicked herself overboard. It wouldn't have surprised him if she had nightmares—if not about the litto, then about the previous events of the day.

He couldn't understand what had happened at the casino. He had worried about his inability to stop when he needed to, but it was the clearest and most controlled he had ever felt while gambling. And he knew the reason was Sonia—focusing on her presence quieted the part of his mind that said *more, more, more,* and left behind *her, her,*

her. Stopping wasn't an issue; even when he was taken to the private game, being able to watch her through the gap in the guards was all he needed to stay in control of himself.

Until that yreet. Seeing his hand on her thigh made Haez's blood boil, even with her redirecting the touch. He could have gone longer, and the sharks at the table had been griping as he'd started to gather his winnings. But his mind was clear. It was time to stop for both of them. They would find a lead on a transport another way—one that wouldn't have strangers pawing at Sonia.

The last thing he remembered was looking up again to see Sonia's heels squeaking uselessly against the polished floor, dragged by the slimeball who was already tenting his pants. The next second, he was covered in blood and looking in her horror-stricken face. She had looked so scared.

Of you, he thought. Thinking about how he might be the fresh subject of her nightmares made his heart clench. And now, she was truly trapped with him until they escaped or died. He was disgusted with himself for feeling a dark curl of pleasure at the thought. It didn't matter how nice she smelled or how infuriatingly cute her smile was or how her hassling felt like home. He didn't deserve her presence. And she didn't deserve any of this.

After his outburst, she would probably want to board whatever transport was going far, far away from him. He wouldn't blame her, but that didn't stop the thought from making him desperately sad. As quietly as he could, he dug a cloth out of his pack and scrubbed the remains of the yellow makeup off his face, along with the lingering splatters of blood. He could only hope that if he changed back to his regular clothes and regular face, it would help him look less like a nightmare when she woke up.

If he was very lucky, maybe he would still look like a friend.

As they descended into the city, the towers became more crowded-together as shorter towers joined the others and narrowed the spaces between them even more. The spokes projecting from each tower dwindled to scrape back a little more space for narrow glider openings in each layer. Eventually, some of the towers were lonely islands only connected to the rest of the web by single walkways and the only open platforms you could see were on rooftops.

Each layer was less populated than the last, and eventually they reached levels old and deep enough to have long-since been abandoned. As the people thinned, the garbage grew. Detritus from upper levels always fell like rain in Quantrin, either redirected by the grated synthsteel canopies that covered the main spokes or kicked farther down on the uncovered walkways. The weight of time and trash had caused these canopies to collapse onto the paths below, and with no pedestrians to move it along, the garbage built up. It formed thick carpets of old food containers, clothes, and even the occasional glider that must have lost repulsion while parked and drifted down as its owner looked on helplessly. Haez tried to not think about how many bodies must have been buried in the mass. It wasn't hard for a night of drunken celebration to end with someone falling over a railing and not being seen again.

He finally spotted a rooftop with a spot clear enough to land the cart. It impacted with a jostle and crunch that startled Sonia awake. Sure enough, she was wide-eyed and hyperventilating. Haez held out a burgundy hand to calm her.

"It's okay. We just landed."

She didn't recoil from him at least. She looked around at all the garbage and then back up the towers. "Is it nighttime?"

"I don't think any sun makes it down this far. Just tower lights—what's left of them at least." The ever-present stripes of lights that ran up the sides of the skyscrapers still burned, but they were reduced to a sickly green that threatened to flicker out at any second. The thermoelectric conduits at the centre of the towers pulled energy from the planet's core and kept power going toward any level they passed through. It still didn't make up for the disrepair that was slowly breaking down anything too deep to be occupied anymore.

Sonia shivered and climbed out of the cart. "What now?"

"We should hole up and get some rest. Look for somewhere unlocked."

They walked down a walkway that connected their rooftop to a residential tower block, stepping high over the garbage they could pass and muscling what they couldn't off to darker places. Haez walked along the side of the tower and pressed door panels to no avail. Each one he tried was burnt out and nonfunctional. If they were working, all he got were angry red lights. Behind him, he heard the click-and-hiss of old air rushing out. Sonia was standing at the now-open door closest to the walkway, tucking something back into her belt pouches.

He walked back towards her, scratching at the back of his scalp. "I tried that one, didn't I?"

Sonia laughed and weakly wiggled her hands in the air. "Ta-da." Haez huffed a tired chuckle and moved to enter the unit but noticed Sonia staring at their cart.

"Something wrong?" he asked.

Her mouth twisted with uncertainty. "We should bring the cart inside."

"There isn't anyone down here to steal anything."

"I know," she said, still nervous. "I know. I just have a bad feeling about leaving it out."

He was too tired to argue, and at that point, Haez would have been willing to move all the garbage on the level if it would have made Sonia feel better. She had seen enough today, and she deserved some peace of mind. He nodded and they went back down the walkway. Sonia retrieved the cart while Haez kicked the path clear ahead of her. He was sweating new stains into his fancy shirt by the time they were able to push the cart through the door.

The inside of the unit was like a time capsule. Everything was at least a century out of date and immaculately preserved. Sonia was immediately transfixed. Once the cart was safely inside, she went wandering further into the home, running her hands over these relics from someone else's life. Haez slid the door shut and locked it behind them. There wasn't anyone down here, but Sonia wasn't the only one with a twisting gut feeling.

He went to the mantle over an ancient terminal and picked up one of the photos on display. An elderly couple had lived there. They'd probably been some of the last people on this level, and when they died, the home remained vacant.

He was embarrassed at how quickly his mind homed in on the fact that it was a mephite and a human in the photos. The man had the same harshly angled bone structure as Haez, but his age showed in his flaky horns and faded grey skin. He and his wife smiled at each other blissfully and Haez wondered what she would look like if her pale-blue eyes were replaced with a deep brown. Maybe smiling at a face of ashy red.

What the fuck is wrong with you, he thought, shoving the photo back on the mantle and rubbing his fingers into his eyes like he could gouge the musing out of his brain. If she could have heard his obsessive thoughts, she'd have been running for the hills. Around him, the lights suddenly snapped to life. Sonia looked up from the wall panel she had been fiddling around in and gave a satisfied nod. Haez moved away from the photos, hoping she wouldn't look for herself and notice what he had been staring at. Her attention was thankfully drawn to a set of shelves tucked into the corner of the room.

"Wow, real flex books," she breathed, pulling one down from the shelf and carefully easing it open. Haez looked over her shoulder at them.

"Have you ever seen them before?" he asked. Sonia nodded, not looking up from the pages.

"When I was a kid. My grandma used to collect them. This is the first time I've ever actually held one instead of looking through a flexiglass case." she chuckled, not looking up from the book. "I think she just collected them because it made her feel worldly. She spent too much time watching daytime holos to read any. She'd make me watch them with her and I'd never know what was going on because she wouldn't stop ranting about everyone's performances."

"What happened to her?" Haez asked. Sonia tensed and slid the book back into place.

"She died," she said firmly. *Sensitive topic, got it,* he thought.

"My mom collects them too. Reads them in the garden while Ma is weeding. She insists that you can't read old stories in a modern format."

Sonia brightened at that. "A garden? Like a real garden?" With a teasing smile, she added, "Are you rich or something? If you've been secretly rich this whole time, I'll be very upset."

Haez gave a sharp laugh. "Not so much. I'm from Ghusn, it's a forest world. Most people at least have a little greenery of their own."

Her smile became dreamy at the thought. "A whole world of trees, huh?"

He nodded, mirroring her beatific expression. "Yeah. It's beautiful. At least it was when I was there last. That's probably where I'm going after all this is over." He thought back to her cagey reaction to how she came to be on Quantrin, and how the dead grandmother had been the first family she'd been willing to acknowledge. Tentatively, he continued, "Do you know where you're going?"

She was silent for a long time before she quietly said, "I'm pretty tired. We should get some sleep and figure things out in the morning." She awkwardly gestured to an open door behind them. "The bedroom is through there. There's enough room for both of us if you want."

Haez shook his head. "I'll be okay with the couch. You get some rest." Sonia relaxed and muttered a goodnight. He could live with one night of a stiff back if it meant Sonia could sleep a bit easier. He wasn't sure how he would handle it if she woke up from a nightmare and realized that the blood-covered monster was lying next to her.

No, the couch would do. Haez turned down the lights and dug his coat out of the cart to use as a blanket. As he drifted off to sleep, he dreamed of Sonia in a garden.

· · · ● · ● · ● · · ·

"Haez?"

The panicked whisper cut through his dreaming of books and flowers and honey-coloured skin. He jerked awake to Sonia standing over him, finger pressed to her lips and eyes glued to the door. He was about to ask her what the problem was when he heard it.

Scratching. Snuffling. Something outside the door.

Haez gently grabbed her shoulders and guided her to sit beside him on the couch. He leaned to whisper in her ear, "The door's locked. It can't get in."

"*It?* No one should be living down here, right?"

"I don't know," he replied. It was half-true. Nothing should have been living at these levels. But there had always been rumors, ones he had dismissed as cautionary tales to deter reckless kids from doing exactly what they had done. And yet, something very real was pawing at the door frame, looking for whatever had left the smell of life in the area.

They clenched each other's hands and waited for the scratching creature to grow bored and wander away. When the noises faded out to silence, Haez sighed and patted Sonia on the hand.

"It's gone now. You should get back to sleep."

Sonia stood but didn't let go of his hand. "I don't want to be alone right now. If that's okay."

More than okay. Haez nodded and stood, letting Sonia lead him back to a bedroom still decorated to the tastes of centuries-past grandparents. She lay on her side in a curled ball and reached a hand back to him. He settled in behind her and drew her back against his chest. Before long, her breathing slowed and evened out. Haez fought sleep as long as he could, hypervigilant and listening for more ominous sounds from the door. Eventually, the sweet smell of Sonia's hair overwhelmed his paranoia and he drifted back into dreams.

• • • ●• • ● • • •

In the morning, Sonia was gone. Haez woke slowly and tried to reach for her warmth only to have his hand scratch against the neatly folded piece of flex she left on her pillow. Half awake, he opened it and squinted at the scratchy writing.

Don't leave, don't follow me. I'll be back.

It jolted him awake. He jumped out of the bed and ran through the unit, sticking his head through every door. "Sonia?! Sonia!"

Nothing. He finally slid open the front door and looked out onto the garbage-strewn level. One of the broken-down gliders that had been resting on an adjacent rooftop was missing, and based on how many paths had been knocked clear of garbage, it was a rough ride going back up. He had a good idea of where she had gone.

Oh, Sonia. What have you done?

11

Sonia

They needed Ottok. Sonia understood Haez's concerns. She didn't even disagree with them. But they were out of options. They could only run away deeper and deeper into the city for so long until they were caught and killed either by the Sabres or something hungrier. The thought of the scratching at the door sent shivers down her spine. But Ottok was smart; he was connected. If there were anyone left who could get them off planet, Ottok would know.

After Haez had fallen asleep, she slid out from under his arm and left the note for him. She took a minute to admire his face and put a hand over his sunken cheek. He looked peaceful. *Please don't hate me for this*, she thought. She went into his bag of clothes and layered herself until her body was a shapeless block, unidentifiable to anyone who may be watching for her sturdy form.

The door slid open and shut as quiet as a whisper when she slunk out of the home. The pathway that wrapped around the outside of the tower had been cleared of trash by whatever had come sniffing around in the night. The cleared trail disappeared around the far corner of the tower and out of sight. She prayed that it was far away by now and stepped carefully to one of the abandoned gliders, not wanting to disturb the garbage and risk drawing attention.

The glider was in decent repair, other than the frayed wiring of the repulsors. It only took a few minutes of work before it was crackling and whirring to life. She had never flown a glider before, and it took a few minutes of wobbling and veering into the garbage piles before she got the hang of it. Finally, she trusted herself enough to carefully steer the glider up through the gaps in the level walkways. She only took it as far as she needed to get to a level serviced by public transit, where she abandoned it underneath a secluded back walkway and rode the earthworms up to familiar paths.

She almost forgot how clear the air felt at that elevation. When she first came to Quantrin, the atmosphere tasted like ash and ozone. Now, as the shorter towers fell away and made space for wind again, it was the sweetest thing she had ever smelled. Seeing the bridges and platforms jammed with people—regular people and not criminals or monsters—felt like a sight from a lifetime ago. When she disembarked at Ottok's level, surrounded by people who used to be neighbors on walkways that used to feel like home, it struck her all at once that she really needed her dad.

At first, she tried to walk and not draw attention, but as she neared Ottok's residential block, she couldn't help breaking into a run, letting the flex and bounce of the grated synthsteel underfoot propel her forward. Before she knew it, she was on the path under his window, her hands digging into the familiar fingerholds. Hopefully he'd left the window open for her.

Gripping the bottom of the window frame, she pulled herself up enough to peek inside: the same clutter as usual, but no sign of Ottok. Usually at this time, he would be puttering around, cursing at the self-made mess, and nursing a morning brew to chase away the hangover from his evening brew. Not today. Even the mess seemed more tame than usual.

She angled her head to look for the distortion of a holoshield. Nothing—he must have left the window open for her after all. She pulled gently at the flexiglass and it swung quietly on its hinges. With the window open, the silence was even more striking.

"Ottok?" she called quietly. No response. She climbed the rest of the way in and carefully pulled the flexiglass closed behind her. Her nerves were getting to her—no way he could have even heard a little peep like that. She cleared her throat and tried again.

"Ottok! Ottok? You here, Dad?" she yelled, casual as possible. Nothing was wrong. Even Haez admitted that there wasn't anything connecting Ottok to the robbery.

Unless there was. What if—

A thump. A shuffle. Something moved in the adjoining room. Sonia dropped down behind a table and peered out at the doorway. She fucked up. Something is wrong. She missed something. The monster followed her here. She—

Into the room stumbled Ottok. A little tired and worn-down-looking, but just Ottok. Sonia stood slowly and sighed with relief.

"Hi," she breathed, eyes watering already. Ottok gave a grimacing smile.

"Sit down before you fall down, kiddo. We gotta talk."

· · · • · • · • · · ·

For the first time in days, Sonia felt relaxed. She hunched down on one of the squat stools that faced onto Ottok's tiny kitchen nook while sipping a mug of steaming beanta. The cheap metal cup made it taste metallic in her mouth, just like Ottok's beanta always did. Even if it woke her up the same, beanta just didn't taste right if it didn't have that slightly-off tang.

While Ottok puttered around gathering whatever food happened to be in the back of his cupboards, Sonia took in the comforting familiarity of his unit. It was nearly as cluttered as Sonia's, with every bit of scrap and machinery that he couldn't bring himself to discard scattered across the surfaces. The only real bits of softness were the stools and the utilitarian cot he had tucked in the tiny closet where he slept. He would joke that he didn't take up much space and the tools needed their breathing room, but she knew the real reason was because it was the only place in his unit that got warm enough that his joints wouldn't ache through the damp Quantrin nights.

Ottok slid her a bowl half-filled with salted seed clusters. "Sorry, it's all I have," he grumbled. "Staukar's men were here sniffing around the morning after you pulled the job. I spent the next day clearing out the bugs. Haven't left since." He sat down on a stool facing Sonia across the kitchen bar and fell into rubbing at the piercings across his beak. Finally, he sighed, "Damn it, Sonia, what in the hells happened? How did we miss this?"

"Rakir set up Haez," she said, setting down her mug. "There wasn't anything in the intel. We only got out of there because Haez figured it out."

"So he *was* there? Did he try anything?"

Sonia's face heated, remembering that night in the mansion, and she took another drink from her mug to hide her expression. "No. We're hiding out on one of the abandoned levels. We need transport off planet. We had to sell a bit of the haul, but we can still barter with the rest. Do you know anyone who can help us?"

"Maybe for you. They've gotten wind that a human was involved, but they don't have a name yet. Haez is the one they were asking after. He's too risky to move." When Sonia gave him a hard stare, he continued, "Don't give me that look. I've done enough for Haez and nothing good has come from it. He can rot for all I care."

Sonia stood and paced the room. She stopped in front of an array of photos pasted to a wall and partially blocked by piles of scrap. They depicted dozens of kids, teens, and young adults. Some were of them smiling with their arms slung over Ottok's shoulder, some just existing in the Quantrin cityscape, some sitting at the same kitchen bar in the workshop. It didn't take much scanning to spot one of Haez, looking younger than she was now and still lanky with youth. It was jarring to see him with both horns and a wide, innocent smile across his face. He was definitely already an adult in the picture but knowing him now made it look like a childhood photo.

There were more—one with the Delnul brothers, no more than fifteen and eating noodles on the same squat stools that lay behind her. One with the only thin yreet Sonia had ever seen, dangling by one of his four hands out the window frame she had just climbed in. His face was so full of laughter she could almost hear it. And countless more that she had never seen before. Almost all of them already wore the thin bracelets marking them as indentured, either in Sabre gold or another gang's colours.

None of the pictures showed her. Even in his personal mementos, Sonia was kept isolated from the rest of Ottok's strays. Based on the dust, it had been years since a photo had been added to the array.

Over her shoulder, Sonia said, "We went to *The Celeste*, Dad." At Ottok's silence, she turned back to face him. He was staring down at the mug clutched in his own hands, talons nervously tapping the metal. She took a deep breath and continued, "Why didn't you tell me? About any of it?"

Ottok was quiet for a long time before saying, "You were lucky, Sonia. When I found you, it was a miracle that someone else hadn't already offered you a contract in exchange for a few hot meals. Most of the kids I found were already trapped. I just tried to help them survive it. But you . . . you could have escaped. I wanted so damn much for you to get out of it."

"Well, maybe I would have tried harder to if I had known," she snapped. "Instead, I've spent seven fucking years playing dress up and dreaming that one day I could be a famous burglar. That's why you never wanted me to meet any of your contacts, right? Because they'd try to get me in the exact same position as everyone else down in that hellhole."

Ottok winced at her tone. She sighed and tried to soften her voice before continuing. "I'm sorry. It's just that I thought I knew what my life was going to look like—"

"—and now you know where that road ends," Ottok finished for her. "With a little gold bracelet."

Sonia nodded and stayed silent, her lips pressed tight with the effort to not cry. Ottok stood and shuffled to stand next to her, looking at the photos. After a moment, he pointed out a picture tucked towards a lower corner.

"That was Thrass," he said, tapping on the face of a surly young wiloh. "They were a good kid. Wanted to get a job on a freighter and get out of here." He moved his talon to point to the platinum bracelet on their wrist. "They got roped in with the Quasars, though. Only made it a few rotations as a fixer before pissing off the boss. People were finding pieces of them for weeks."

Ottok pulled his hand back and folded his arms in front of his body. "They were all like that. Just kid after kid that I had to watch end up dead. I should have told you. But . . . hells, I don't know. Maybe you weren't the only one playing make-believe. Maybe I just wanted to pretend that you could live your life without having that hanging over your head. It was selfish, but you deserved a better life than Quantrin had to offer."

"We all did," she said quietly, letting her gaze linger on Thrass. "And now I don't have any choice—I have to leave the planet. I'm twenty-five with nowhere to go and no skills other than scamming and stealing. What the fuck am I going to do, Ottok?"

"You're going to survive, kiddo," he said, a hint of pride in his voice. "Stars know, you're too stubborn to do anything else."

A chuckle left Sonia and the smallest hint of a smile crept into her face. She nodded in agreement and returned to the short stool. "Can't argue with that."

"That's the spirit. Now, I can think of six transports that might be able to move you—" Ottok started while retrieving a pad of flex from a nearby drawer. Sonia cut him off.

"Both of us. I'd be dead if it weren't for Haez. I owe him."

Ottok gave her a suspicious look, one that made her feel like he was looking straight through her brain and into her soul. It was true that she owed Haez, and it was also true that she liked the way he smiled and how he made her feel safe even when he was fucking her like he hated her and how much he seemed to like her when she was just being Sonia.

She still wanted to hear him call her a good girl again. The memory of his hand on hers and those two words made her face heat and her stomach flutter.

"Fine," Ottok said, "but that's only going to leave you with two. There's one leaving from dock 59 in five days. The captain owes me and he won't ask questions, but you'll have to come back up to the port levels. It could be dicey. The other is in ten days from a shadow port on the planet's surface. Right on the edge of the wastes."

The second option filled Sonia with dread twice-over. The wastes were a section of city that had collapsed in on itself a millennium past, back when the city was still growing and had yet to test the limits of its strength. The bent and broken conduits inside the collapsed towers created enough radiation that it was still too dangerous to be repaired or cleared. Instead, the city built the remaining towers with micrograv emitters embedded in the walls to prevent another catastrophe, and the wastes were forgotten.

But the criminals didn't forget. Anyone coming into Quantrin who didn't want to be noticed would enter over the wastes and stay there as long as possible before going to their destination. The radiation scrambled scanners badly, so smugglers, criminals, and even a slim few who were too cheap to pay for docking clearance would risk the side-effects. But most people weren't going any deeper than the occupied levels.

No one was really sure what was on the planet's surface, just that no one went there except for a handful of spacers who operated the shadow ports. They would only ever stay for a few days at a time before leaving the planet again, never interacting directly with their contacts. Sending out deliveries meant summoning one of their drones to traverse the levels and retrieve your shipment. Sonia had seen Ottok use them a few times, where a drone with a bundle strapped to its belly would beep outside his window until he let it in. After he unstrapped his delivery, he would replace it with whatever an off-world contact had requested, along with a loaded credit chit.

Nobody knew if they'd paid enough until they got confirmation from the recipient. If they hadn't, they would never see their shipment again. It was a risky way to move anything, and even someone as seasoned as Ottok only used it for transporting his dirtiest work—illegal weapon modifications, custom surveillance gear, couldn't risk being intercepted by the law. It was risky, dangerous, and above all, discreet—if Ottok had managed to track down the exact location of a port, they certainly wouldn't have scruples about moving wanted criminals.

But Sonia remembered the scratching at the door.

"No," she said, "we'll make it to dock 59."

Ottok nodded and started making notes on the flex. "You're going to look for Captain Tharon of the Dark Dusk. The ship name is stupid as spit, but tell him you like it. He's a thin-skinned son of a bitch." He produced a credit chit and pressed it against his wristcom until it chirped to indicate deposited funds. "Give him that and tell him that his ionising converter is on me."

He thought for a moment and jotted down another block of information. "For my peace of mind," he said, seeing Sonia's pinched expression. When he passed the flex across the narrow table, she looked it over while worrying the corner.

"You should come with us," she said. "If Staukar finds out that you helped us—"

"I'll be fine. Old Ottok has been through worse than this," he replied with a placating nod. "I sure hope that dirtbag is worth all this trouble."

"Yeah, me too."

Just as Sonia was about to take another sip of her beanta, a banging knock cut through the calm. Both she and Ottok tensed and went wide-eyed at the angry voices outside his unit.

"You found all the bugs, right?" Sonia asked in a rush. Ottok nodded sharply.

"Of course I did. What the hells are they after now?"

After another set of pounding knocks, a singular voice cut through the indecipherable chatter. "Open up, Ottok. We know you got Haez's bitch in there."

Electric terror shot through Sonia. She jumped to her feet in a panic.

"You came through the window, didn't you?" Ottok asked. When Sonia nodded, he rushed to push open the window and looked at the frame. He cursed. "Motion sensors. They must have climbed up and placed them after they left the last time."

Sonia had already started shoving the flex and credit chit into her layers of clothing and Ottok frantically rummaged in a box, dumping half the contents on the floor. He finally produced a lumpy-looking belt and shoved it to Sonia.

"Emergency chute. Don't try to get to transit, just jump to the next level and run."

She strapped it tight around her waist without argument. She hesitated before going to the window and gave Ottok a desperate look, her tears blurring him out.

Please. Please, Dad, come with me. She couldn't say it out loud. This escape was going to be hell even for her, let alone for an old gallan with stiff joints. Easily reading her thoughts through her eyes, he shook his head. His expression was sad and resigned. "There's nothing for it now, kid. You gotta get going."

Sonia still rushed towards him, threw her arms around him as far as they would reach and buried her face in his feathery shoulder. He stiffened for a moment before hugging her back tight enough to make her think that maybe she could stay.

"I'm so sorry, Dad," she whispered. "Thanks for taking care of me. For everything." She waited for his usual grumble and sigh, but he just squeezed her back tighter.

"Keep yourself safe. For my sake."

She nodded against his shoulder before pulling back. There was another bang at the door, now sounding like someone was trying to kick it down. Drifting up through the window were mirrored shouts of Sabres blocking her escape. Let the bastards try.

She ran for the window and dove through into the open air. For a moment, everything hung still in tableau. Behind her, Ottok reactivated the holoshielding as his unit was stormed. A stun blast from below grazed her foot and knocked out feeling up to her knee. Her momentum carried her past the edge of the walkway under Ottok's window and held her suspended against gravity.

Then the freefall dragged her down and brought time back in a rush.

The city lights rose around her as she picked up speed, the glowing spots streaking into neon teeth. They closed over head as she barreled down into the city's maw. She passed safely between walkways of one, two, three levels before realizing that a platform was rushing up to meet her, the grated floor ready to split her to pieces. She waited until the last possible second to activate the emergency chute and the belt stopped her momentum so suddenly that it lurched up and threatened to crack her ribs. Still, it allowed her to gently touch down on the synthsteel before the Sabres would've even had a chance to open the doors to their gliders. By the time they were taking off to search, she was gone.

You found a fucking transport, alright, she thought bitterly as she limped through a back lane towards the nearest transit station. She wanted to cling to a thread of hope that maybe Haez was wrong—maybe Ottok's wits and connections could keep him safe. She wanted to believe she hadn't just doomed the only person on Quantrin who ever cared about her.

But Haez was right about one thing: she was smarter than that.

· · · · · ● · ◉ · ● · · ·

Sonia hardly knew how long it took to get back to Haez. She'd meant to ride the worms back down to the level where she left the glider, but her light-headedness and nausea almost made her lose her grip. She only made it a few levels before having to shamble away from the transit station and look for another glider to boost. Her trip down was a glazed-over blur, only punctuated by having to nestle the glider against the underside of a walkway to rest briefly—only long enough for a nap. Any more than that and her thoughts threatened to strangle her with tears.

When she finally returned to the trash level, she parked the glider in the cleared spot. Her body was weak with exhaustion as she shuffled to the door, the sensation finally returning to her leg. She could only hope that Haez hadn't locked her out.

He hadn't. The second the door slid open, and he was on her, grasping her biceps and shoving her against the wall.

"What did you do?!" he yelled in her face. At first, she didn't reply, hunching down to stare at her feet and hide her swollen eyes. He shook her by the shoulders to make her focus. "You went to Ottok, didn't you?"

She gave a small nod and quietly said, "Staukar's men came. Ottok made me run. I . . . I don't know what happened to him."

"I told you this would happen!" he shouted, giving her another shake. "What were you thinking?!"

She knocked his hands off her, tears finally forcing themselves through. "I know I fucked up, okay? But no one else would have helped us."

"We were going to figure it out together! Now Ottok might be dead because you were lazy!"

A flame of anger ripped through the ashes that filled her head, consuming her in an instant. She pulled back and slammed a fist into his jaw, knocking him sideways into the wall.

"Fuck you!" she screamed. "Fuck you, fuck you, fuck you, you rancid asshole!"

"What happened to figuring it out in the morning?" He roared back, shoving himself up and balling his own fists. "Were you always planning to go? Hells, it's like lying is a hobby for you!"

She winced back from the comment which stabbed like a needle into a wound she didn't know was still raw. Quietly, she replied, "You wouldn't have let me go if you knew."

"Damn right, I wouldn't have," he said. He rubbed his hands over his face. "Did you at least get a lead?"

"Yes," she said with a nod. "It leaves from dock 59 in five days."

"Fine. Five days. After that, we're through."

With that, Haez stormed for the door, snatching up his coat as he went.

"Haez, wait—" she croaked, but he didn't stop, letting the door slide shut behind him. All alone, she collapsed in a heap on the floor, her hands balled painfully in her own hair and her wailing sobs filling the deathly silent unit. Ottok would have been embarrassed with them both—fighting at a time like this.

I guess it doesn't matter what Ottok thinks anymore.

12

Haez

It took hours of Haez walking the garbage-blocked paths before he could even hear past the blood pounding in his ears. He started screaming out at the echoing towers and kicking piles of garbage off to the deeper layers. He found an old pipe and took it up like a club, smashing at everything he could. Anything to vent the rage.

Ottok might have been done with Haez, but that didn't change the fact that he'd only survived the planet because the old gallan had taken pity on a freshly indentured kid. He loved Ottok—everyone did. How many others had only survived the Quantrin meat grinder because Ottok had looked out for them? How many times had Ottok pulled Haez back from the brink of destitution?

Ottok was special—he cared. And if he died, no one else could or would fill his place. No one would get pulled back anymore.

Staukar wouldn't kill him, at least not right away. But the goodwill that Ottok held within the underworld would only protect him for so long. After that, it would depend on how long it took for Staukar to wretch every secret he could from the old man's beak.

Eventually the world came back to Haez—the damp creeping through his coat, the occasional drip of water splatting on his scalp and running down under his collar, the stench of a few centuries' worth of garbage. When he was clear-headed enough to feel un-comfortable about how sticky the bottoms of his boots felt, he went back.

The glider that Sonia had stolen was the one good thing to come out of the situation. It must have belonged to a young guy preparing for a weekend of partying, since the back was laden down with bags upon bags of salty snacks and enough liquor to put a block party into a collective coma. He took everything in with him; stars knew, he could use a drink. Hopefully it would be enough to last until their transport—five days were all they needed.

The door slid open, and at first, all he saw was the empty living room. He nearly turned around to see if she had left to pace the walkways when he heard a quiet sniffling. When he took a few steps in, he saw Sonia curled up on the floor with her back to the side of the couch. He walked over and sat down behind her.

"Hey," he said, and immediately wanted to kick himself. A big blowout fight like that and he had 'hey'. Brilliant. Stunning.

"Hey," she replied, voice hoarse from crying. Looking down over her shoulder, Haez saw she was turning something over in her hands that looked like a kebab skewer.

"Don't take this the wrong way, but you might need something bigger than that if you want to get back at me."

She snorted and smiled a little. "I don't know, Haez. I might be *real* determined." Her smile faltered, staring at the skewer in her hand. "This was the first thing Ottok ever gave to me. My grandma raised me until she died. I was seventeen. I had to go back to my user parents and the first thing they did was ditch me in a back lane on Quantrin. I'd been digging around the trash for food and sleeping under heat vents for a month before I met him. He gave me food and put me up in my own unit for a year, but you know Ottok. He always wanted to make sure everyone could take care of themselves.

"So, he gave me this," she said, giving the skewer a twirl between her fingers. "He was the one who showed me how to use one of these to pop the emergency release on old doors. Didn't even damage the lock so you couldn't tell anyone had been in. Anything I could steal, he would help me fence. It worked. I was able to start paying for my own unit. I had a life. He gave me a life when my parents couldn't even be bothered to try selling me for another fix. They just cut off the dead weight. Ottok was a better parent than either of them."

Her face twisted with the effort of not crying again. "And now he's dead. I killed my dad."

He reached a hand down to squeeze her shoulder. She clutched onto it and pressed it against her face.

"We don't know that. Ottok has a lot of goodwill, especially within the Sabres. Even for Staukar, it would be a risky move. And you couldn't have known this would happen."

"You did."

He slid down to the ground to sit beside her and pulled her into a tight hug. She didn't say anything, just shuddered and cried against his chest.

"Maybe. I don't know. If it were me and I knew it would be the last time I saw my parents, maybe I would have risked it too. But whatever happens to Ottok isn't your fault. It's on Staukar."

She didn't have any response to that other than clinging closer. He squeezed her and pressed his nose into her hair, breathing in deep. Even now, cloaked in their mutual anguish, she smelled like honey and hope. He waited until her breathing stabilized before speaking again.

"I need to know you aren't going to lie to me anymore. I know we both get through life on lies, but we aren't going to get through this one unless we can trust each other. I want to feel like I can trust you," he said quietly. It felt so good to be holding her and a small part of him still feared she would smirk and tell him he was an idiot for believing this could be real.

But she didn't. She just nodded and pulled back.

"No more lying," she rasped in agreement. "Not even for dealing with other people. It's too confusing."

"Confusing?"

Her tawny cheeks flushed prettily, and she looked down to the ground.

"You know what I mean."

He wasn't going to let her off the hook that easily. He turned to face her while she still avoided eye contact.

"I'm not the first chump you pulled the innocent little girl bit with. Why is it confusing now?"

"Haez," she warned, her cheek's glow deepening to a lurid blush. He traced a finger along her jawline to turn her face towards his.

"No lying, right?" he whispered, leaning in towards her. Her eyes were wide and nervous.

Finally, she leaned forward and pressed her lips to his. Every time they kissed had felt different, but this was the first time it felt nervous, careful, and . . . honest. Her lips were softer than silk and still trembling slightly.

They parted to look at each other, a silent question hanging in the air of what came next. They agreed together and dove back on each other, kisses turning ravenous. Their tongues twined together as Sonia climbed into his lap, only breaking apart so they could pull at each other's clothing. Haez yanked the layers away from Sonia's body and descended on her bare shoulder and neck, kissing marks onto her skin. She arched her back and grasped his horn to keep him in place, gasping at the sensations.

Haez felt heat roaring through him at her taste, her smell, her everything. Every fibre of his being was made of need. He was crushing her to his body when she gasped out, "Haez, are . . . are you okay? You're . . . *really* red."

The fraction of his brain that was still sensible pulled him back to look at her breathless face and then down at his own hands. She was right. The usual burgundy was flaring to a bright, clear crimson. All at once, pieces fell into place.

Shit, not now, he thought, watching the red spreading over his body. He knew what was happening—what had been happening.

Sonia was in danger.

13

Sonia

Haez abruptly pushed Sonia off him and jumped to his feet. She protested as he rushed around the room, snatching up a bag of food.

"Haez, what the hell was that?" she asked as his head whipped around the room. He finally looked at the washroom and unceremoniously threw the food inside. Without making eye contact, he started talking at her.

"Sonia, this is very important. I'm going to go in there and you need to short out the panel so it locks behind me. Whatever happens, you don't come in here."

"But—"

"Just trust me. Please." He gave her a pleading look, tension laced through his body. She was silent for a moment before breathing her agreement. He gave her a pained smile before rushing into the washroom and letting the door slide shut behind him. Sonia jumped into action, popping the panel and pulling a couple wires that would prevent the door from being opened from the inside. The panel flashed an angry red, and as the power blinked out, she heard muffled grunts and groans filtering through the door along with the slap of flesh on flesh.

She was stunned speechless. One second, he was kissing her with the promise of fucking all the grief away, and the next she was standing like a dope while he jacked off on the toilet. She wandered away from the door and plopped down on the couch in a dumbfounded haze. To her own surprise, she laughed; quiet, rueful chuckles at first, then wheezing, unhinged cackles. What else could she do?

"I hate my life," she said to herself, hearing Haez give an anguished moan through the door. Not much she could do but rest. Certainly, things would seem better after some sleep.

• • • ● • ● • • • •

Things were not better after sleep. Sonia naively hoped that she would go to bed and wake to hear Haez knocking on the bathroom door and sheepishly asking to be let out. Instead, she was woken by his muffled whining, even more desperate and needy than before. That couldn't be normal.

Exercise always cleared her mind. She did what she could without leaving the unit. The near constant noises from the washroom were hard to tune out, but it was still better than risking whatever might have been scuttling around outside.

After an hour, the film of anxiety smothering her thoughts had been cleared away. The terminal looked to be in decent repair and when she wriggled underneath and opened up the innards, it only took a few minutes of tightening loose wires to get it back online. She needed to find out what was going on. Retrieving one of the mystery drinks brought in from the glider, she curled into a creaking chair and got to work.

Haez's noises blended into the background as Sonia dove into the holonet, trying to find anything to shed some light on their situation. She spent hours digging into medical resources before she found her answer, and when she did, it was like the puzzle of his behaviour came together with a snap.

The mephites called it *bytrr*. There wasn't a translation to standard—it was considered incredibly crass to discuss it even with other mephites, let alone chatting about it with other races. The closest approximation was some sort of rut that men would enter, only every few years and woefully unpredictably. Usually there were some signs before it started, but they could be hard to spot if you didn't know what you were looking for. Haez was older than her, but not by much. It might have only happened to him once or twice before.

Suddenly everything made sense—his outburst at the casino, the weird possessive behavior, the sniffing. Most would be irritable and wound-up for a few days beforehand. If they had a romantic partner or interest, it could be much, much worse—bashing a bloody dent into a yreet's skull was almost mundane in context. She wasn't sure how that made her feel. It was flattering to know that on some level, he did reciprocate her feelings, if they were real feelings at all. Maybe their meeting along with the timing of his *bytrr* had tricked him into thinking that she was worth his affection.

Sonia gave herself a shake. It wasn't the time to worry about whether or not the guy jacking off on the washroom floor thought she was pretty. They had four days left until their transport. She needed to know how long this thing was going to last.

The question was easier asked than answered. Some sources said it could resolve in a day, others said weeks. The only thing they did agree on was that enduring it alone would make it last longer. But even having a companion might only spare a few days and then they would both be trapped—a man in the thick of his *bytrr* wasn't likely to give up his partner, even if the ordeal ran dangerously long.

As soon as she started looking for information on the *bytrr* by name, it became impossible to avoid the porn that got thrown in her face. Despite most mephites wanting to keep this inconvenient species quirk to themselves, there were enough who chose to capitalize on it to have made them popular with certain groups of perverts.

Including me, I guess. She clicked on one of the videos.

The woman was a wiloh with electric-green skin and long head-tendrils bound into a massive bun. She was relaxing on a bed when her partner entered, a mephite man close to Haez's height and puffy with glamour muscles. The intense flush of *bytrr* had turned his skin the same bright red that Haez's had taken on when he'd sealed himself away. As soon as he entered the room, the wiloh started moaning and arching like he was already balls-deep inside her. Sonia rolled her eyes. How ridiculous.

Right?

She focused on the man as he started to undress, hardly able to stop groping at his own cock through his clothing. When he finally freed his length, Sonia had to pause the video. She gaped at it and her jaw went slack. It had to be a porn thing. It wasn't like all human men looked like porn actors. But there were mentions of . . . physical changes associated with *bytrr*. When Haez fucked her, it already felt like he was rearranging her insides with every thrust. And if that was among the changes? Well, Sonia was feeling very, very small because that cannon between the actor's legs was very, very large.

If Haez wasn't mentally able to exercise restraint and he was wielding something like that, she could get seriously hurt. And for days on end, no less—couldn't someone die from that? Suddenly the fear and worry on Haez's face before sealing himself away made sense. She wasn't sure if she should feel happy that he put her safety first or scared of the possibility of him deciding that he didn't want to go it alone after all. The door was strong, but it was for a toilet. It wasn't exactly designed to hold up against a home invasion.

On cue, there was a roar of frustration from the other room followed by silence. She hoped he was sleeping. *Maybe I could just take a peek.*

No, she berated herself. He was her friend, not a zoo animal. She would respect his wishes. For now, at least. Until then, she pushed away her curiosity about what she would find inside.

Four days left.

• • • ● • ● ● • • •

Two days passed. Sonia had set the terminal to news broadcasts and the only thing marking the passage of time was the roll of late-night installations to the early-morning talk shows. On the second day, one of the news programs finally made mention of the altercation outside Ottok's residential block. The chief of police held a news conference asking the public for information regarding his kidnapping. It didn't make Sonia feel better, but it at least loosened the knot of anxiety that had made a home in her gut. If nothing else, Ottok's good graces in the community deemed the commotion a high-priority investigation. Kidnapped wasn't dead after all, and if anyone could find him and take the Sabres to task, she would put her money on the steely-eyed police captain. Even through a screen, the woman made Sonia feel guilty for having ever violated the law.

It still did little to distract from the near-constant groaning from the washroom, only broken when Haez's exhaustion forced him to sleep. When he woke, the noises would start again, with his guttural moans eventually morphing into raw-throated wailing as more hours ticked past.

Sonia lay awake on the couch. Part of her wanted to be between the washroom and the apartment exit in case one of the things that scratched around the outside tried to get in. Mostly, she didn't want to feel alone and the thought of what was happening in that room refused to leave her mind.

It's just sex, she kept thinking. What was the worst that could happen? She'd survived Haez's hate-fucking just fine. It couldn't be any worse than that.

And it was taking too long. She might not have been able to comprehend the exact consequences of going in, but she knew the worst case if she didn't. They could miss their transport. They could be stuck down here for weeks. If Staukar talked to the right tech consultant, they might be able to track the lonely terminal that was suddenly back online after a century. If the *bytrr* lasted longer than Haez's food supply, he could die. She would have endangered Ottok for nothing.

An especially tortured moan cut through the air right as there was a moment of silence in the broadcast and Sonia felt a fresh tingle between her thighs.

"Fuck it," she muttered, jerking to her feet. She went back into the bedroom and looked at herself in the full-length mirror beside the door. Her scruffy hair stuck up in all directions and her clothes looked closer to dingy pyjamas. She ran her fingers through her hair to comb it into something civilized-looking and tried to smooth down her shirt. The smoothing turned frantic before she paused and stared herself down in the mirror.

"What the fuck are you doing?" She pulled off the shirt along with the rest of her clothing. Nude in the mirror, she looked herself in the eyes. "You can handle this, Sonia. It's just sex. It's just sex."

The flutter in her stomach kept her from believing herself. She took another steeling breath before charging towards the bathroom door, not giving any more time for second thoughts. She opened the panel and reconnected the wires. It blinked green and she slid the door open.

The heady stink of sweat and cum hit her first, making her reel back from the smell. She wasn't sure what she'd expected to see inside the room, but she was still startled by what greeted her. The room was filled with a miasma that wobbled the air and blurred her view. When she peered through, she could see towels, mats, anything soft that had been left in the washroom had been dragged to the ground and piled into a corner, making a ragged little nest. Someone or something bright-red was curled in the middle. Sonia took a step across the threshold.

"Haez?"

The one-horned thing lifted its head to stare at Sonia and a wave of the miasma washed over her. The force of the clenching in her core dropped her to her knees, suddenly sweating and gasping. "Wha—" she panted, looking up at the form.

The red flush that had started to spread when they were kissing had covered his entire body. Even his eyes were changed, the warm copper glazed over with black.

"Sonia," he growled with a deep reverberation that sent shivers crawling over her skin along with a fresh rush of damp between her legs.

Sonia moaned from the ground. "Haez . . . something . . . something's wrong . . . "

She watched him draw to his full height. From the ground, he looked tall enough for his horns to brush the ceiling and the thick cock looming over her was silhouetted by the overhead lights. She whimpered and crawled towards him, needing his touch more than answers. When she reached him, she wrapped her arms around his leg and craned her head up, trying to steal a taste of his length. Before she could, his hands gripped her biceps and hauled her up off her feet to meet his eyes. They bored into her like twin black holes.

Then he descended, crushing her to his body as his mouth latched onto her neck, kissing and tasting and consuming. Sonia arched her back against him, trying to grind herself down onto his cock. He was too tall for her to reach, so she settled for wrapping her muscled legs around his torso and stealing friction from his stomach. He moaned and pulled her hips in closer.

"What's happening?" she tried again. "I can't think."

He didn't answer. The smell that cloaked the room was even stronger in his arms, like it was seeping out of his pores. Sonia rubbed her nose across the top of his flaming-red scalp, chasing the high of his pheromones.

As quickly as she was brought up, the ground rushed up to meet her as she was thrown down into the nest. Haez descended again, his tongue now sliding up the inside of her leg. The sliver of Sonia that was still coherent enough to be embarrassed tried to pinch her knees together.

"W-wait, Haez—"

He growled and pressed her knees far apart enough to touch the tiles outside the boundary of the towels. Sonia grimaced.

He just needs to get it out of his system she thought to herself. *I can't expect him—*

She was jerked out of her thoughts by Haez pushing his nose to her cunt and breathing deeply. He let out a hoarse moan, followed by the splatter of his cum hitting the floor beneath him. Haez paused, just gasping and taking in her smell.

"Haez?" Sonia tried again. "A-are you—"

"I'm fine," he said, the same reverberation rattling straight through her clit. She shivered at the sensation. "You smell so good."

"How do I help you? What do you need?"

"You," he said, opening his mouth and letting his tongue slide out to tease her clit. "Just you."

Sonia's muscles relaxed as he feasted on her. He wasn't measured or skilled in his ministrations, but his sloppy licks and sucks still had her writhing in the nest and clenching her hand on his horn to keep him in place. The only sounds were their shared gasps and groans and the occasional splat of more cum painting the floor.

She started to quiver helplessly under him as her inevitable peak crawled through her nerves, just waiting to release.

"I'm close," she whimpered, arching off the floor. "Please . . . your fingers—"

She gave a little squeak as Haez circled her twitching cunt with a finger before stretching her with two of them. Together, they were as thick as any human's cock and the promise of having him inside her again was enough to shove her over the edge.

All the pent-up tension in her nerves released as she shook apart under Haez. She was too lost to pleasure to hold back the sharp cry that ripped through her.

And he kept going. Haez's fingers kept her cresting the wave over and over again, not satisfied until her throat was raw from cries and turned into whimpers. She lost count of how many times she climaxed before over-sensitization had her squeezing her knees together and pushing his head back.

Haez sat back on his heels, black eyes still staring holes through her. He wrapped a hand around himself and slowly stroked, never breaking eye contact. For the first time, Sonia was able take in what hung between his legs and felt a flutter of nervousness.

There was no way it had looked like that before. She would have noticed. The thing she was looking at now was closer to the size of her lower arm than anything she had seen on a man. And that girth. She may have been able to get her hand around the shaft, but the head flared so widely that even as pheromone addled as she was, her breath shook with trepidation.

Haez waited and watched as Sonia gaped at his body. She stared as a glossy droplet oozed out of the slit at his tip and slid down that deliciously thick head. That settled it. With a strangled moan, she turned onto her hands and knees, her head lolling as another wave of pheromones made her mind spin.

Sonia pressed her face against the cool tiles, trying to get a little sanity back. Suddenly she felt Haez's hand on her back, sliding up her spine over the corded muscles. She arched into the touch as it stroked back down and grabbed one of her hips. The other was taken in a tight grip. He pushed his thumbs into her lower back, making her hips arch even farther up and forcing her breasts to push down against the floor. It made her feel completely helpless in a way she wanted to last forever.

She caught the sight of the two of them in the large floor-length mirror on the opposite wall. Her eyes were painted over with black just like Haez's, and her mouth hung open limply, a string of drool trailing out and onto the tiles. Haez was pulled tall on his knees behind her, horn silhouetted against the wavering lights, and with his hands bending her hips. His cock was nestled between her ass cheeks and dribbling down her spine. With one of his thumbs, he rubbed a spot into her back just past the tip of the head.

Sonia didn't know if he looked like a demon or a god. Only that she didn't care anymore.

"Please," she whispered under him. "Please please ple—"

She was cut off by a yelp as he lined himself up and started to push. The head stretched her hard and sharp and her mind was stuck between squirming away or pushing back harder against him. Then as quickly as it came, it breeched her with what felt like a tiny pop. Sonia let out a little sigh of relief that the most challenging part was past.

But there was more of him. Now that the thick tip was in her, he started pushing forward with that intimidating length. Sonia cried out again, tears welling up even as her body urged her to take more.

Haez paused, breathing heavily. His eyes squeezed shut and his fists clenched as he tried to slow his breath. His voice seemed to fight against him as he said through clenched teeth, "I can stop." Even as he broke into a sweat, he started to pull out.

The ridge of the wide head dragged against something exquisite inside her. "Ah!" she gasped, "do that again."

"Move?" Haez asked, gently pushing forward again. Sonia moaned in response.

"Fuck, that's . . . . . . so g-good," she panted. Haez growled and gently worked more of his cock into her. Sonia saw stars as the sharply flared edge of his head dragged hard against her g-spot, reducing her to a quivering puddle.

"You like that?" he asked, voice reverberating all around and through them both. Sonia nodded frantically against the tiles.

"Fuck yes, I'm—" she froze mid-sentence. All her muscles tensed, and she let out a scream as she fluttered around him.

"You're so beautiful," he said, picking up his pace ever-so-slightly. "You feel perfect."

Drunk off lust, Sonia blurted, "Am I good?" She was too high from his pheromones to be mortified. Haez nuzzled his sharp nose against the back of her head, taking in her smell.

"So good," he purred. "You're such a good girl. So good for me."

She keened and another gush of slick drenched them both. Haez hunched over so his mouth was next to her ear, never pausing in his gentle, shallow thrusts. He whispered to her over and over about how good she felt and how perfect she was. The reverberation of his voice sent tremors straight to her clit with each affirmation of what a good fucking girl she was. Every word of praise pushed her closer to another crest.

She lifted her head from the floor and braced against her forearms. Haez was being careful to only work part of his length into her. In the reflection, he was soaked with sweat and biting hard on his lip, every ounce of energy spent on controlling himself from hurting his lover. But she wanted more, wanted him to give her everything he had. 'Careful' was gone. Now there was 'need'.

Meeting his thrust with a push of her own, she slammed herself fully back onto Haez's cock with a cry. He let out a roar at the feeling of sinking fully into her body. Any tenuous thread of control he had left was broken. The grip on her hips turned bruising and he started slamming his length into her, met by Sonia's own frantic rocking.

It hurt. Her lust didn't change that she was just too small compared to him in this state. But the delicious feeling of his girth working inside her and the delirious satisfaction that she was taking *all of him* overrode any discomfort. Eventually the pain faded far away leaving only Haez, his divine cock, and the head-spinning high that consumed them both. With the pheromones still swirling in her mind, the added stimulation of his balls slapping against her clit was all she needed to be brought to her peak. Over and over and over she trembled around him.

Haez's grunts got louder and more frantic as he neared his end. "W-where?" he managed.

"Don't stop. Don't you dare fucking stop," Sonia said, clenching around him again.

That was enough to push him over. With another roar, he slammed his hands into the ground on either side of her head and rocked his hips against her. He filled her so much that even though she was impossibly tight around him, she could still feel his cum leaking out around his cock and adding to the mess on the floor. With that image in her mind, one last quivering orgasm twisted through her before she collapsed limply onto the ground.

Haez stayed deep inside her as they both took harsh, panting breaths, trying to recover from their intense peaks. Finally, he drew up slightly and massaged his hands down her back, his palms smoothing over the little bruises blooming on her hips.

"Are you . . . okay?" he asked quietly. Sonia managed a weak nod.

"Better than okay. Are you okay? Feeling normal again?"

Haez let out a low hum and Sonia gasped. He was already stiffening inside her again.

"We should go to the bed. I'm not going to be done with you for a while."

14

Sonia

Time blurred out of focus in Haez's arms. Hours and days dripped off their bodies and into the soup of breath, sweat, and intoxicating pheromones that had taken over the unit. They didn't eat and barely drank, each only sustained by the other's body. When the exhaustion became so much that sleep overtook them, it would only be a few hours before one was waking the other with their roaming tongue and hands. The only thing anchoring Sonia to reality was Haez's mirrored moans as his cock carved out a home inside her. Once the first wave of desperate fucking passed, they were able to be slow and tender. It was the first time she understood what it meant to make love.

When he groaned and spilled in her for the last time, the air in the room became lighter and less oppressive. Finally, his body stopped pumping out the waves of pheromones that had kept them locked together. When he slid out of Sonia and collapsed gasping beside her on the bed, she felt empty. She had almost forgotten what it felt like to not have him inside her and she didn't think anyone but him could fill the space left behind.

Once they both got breath back in their bodies, Sonia looked at Haez and recoiled. His skin had returned to its usual burgundy and his eyes to their warm copper. But his face was a wreck. The contours were always deeply hollowed, but now his skin looked shrunken around his skull. The tight skin pulled his dry, cracked lips back against his teeth. How long had it been since they'd had any water? How had she not noticed him desiccating before her eyes?

Sonia opened her mouth to speak, but a sharp pain suddenly lanced up her spine. A wheezing whimper was all that came out as she curled in around herself, clutching her abdomen. Each second, it grew more intense as the last of the pheromones worked their way out of her system and left behind the harsh physical reality of a human enduring a *bytrr*. She felt bruised from the inside-out, like even the ghost of his length inside her was trying to claw its way free.

Haez held up a hand to her, struggling to his feet and shambling from the room. Even through the blinding pain, she worried over Haez, whose own spine had become prominent enough to count the vertebrae.

He returned with two glasses of water. "Slowly," he croaked, holding one in front of Sonia and guiding a straw to her lips. She took a few small sips in between rattling breaths. When she turned from the water to press her grimacing face into the damp mattress, Haez set aside both glasses and climbed back up beside her on the bed. He gently guided her to lie on her stomach and massaged his thumbs into her lower back. She sighed with relief, even as she trembled from the razor-sharp stabbing in her gut.

"I'm so sorry, Sonia," he murmured, using a hand to comb her hair up and off the cold sweat of her neck before resuming his massaging. "I'm here. You're going to be okay."

She lay prone and shaking, letting Haez rub the agony out of her muscles and brush her hair away from her skin. Finally, the ache subsided enough that she could roll to her side and lift up on an elbow to look at Haez.

"How long?" she rasped. He shook his head with frustration.

"Five days," he said, rubbing his hand over his forehead. "You shouldn't have come in. You should have left me and gotten out."

Sonia didn't reply, instead reaching for her water and taking slow sips while she let this sink in. Five days. Their last chance to get off-planet was gone.

Well, not quite their last. Even as she drank, Sonia felt the ashy feeling coming back into her mouth. Haez started to talk about which docks she should scout to try to get herself off-planet while he figured out his own escape. It blended into a background drone as Sonia shivered, imagining blackness and monsters if they used Ottok's second lead.

She looked at Haez and his drawn face while he rambled about what she could do to save herself—no thinking about his own skin at all. It made up her mind. Either they both left or neither of them did.

"There might be another lead," she said, drawing fully up to sitting. "Ottok mentioned it. We would still have two days."

His brows furrowed when he stared at her. Struggling to keep his voice even, he asked, "Why didn't you tell me this before?"

"It's from the planet's surface, Haez. Edge of the wastes."

His face relaxed and he breathed, "Ah." They both went silent in thought. It was their last shot to get out of there together. But the thought still terrified her. Going down farther into the suffocating black to face who-knows-what felt like volunteering to be buried alive. Haez took one of her hands and said, "Say the word and we forget about it. We can figure out something else."

"What else?" Sonia laughed bitterly. "We're out of choices."

"I know."

"I don't want to go down there, Haez."

He pressed his forehead against hers. "Me neither."

The silence of the room settled like a blanket. They both savoured the last moments of calm before they descended into hell.

• • • • • • • • • •

It took time for them to recover, with them gradually working themselves up to eating and bathing. After five straight days of fucking, sweat, and stink, the shower water ran grey as they gently washed the filth from each other's aching bodies. Once they were hydrated enough that their skin plumped and they no longer trembled to move, they wasted no more time leaving their little haven. Haez pushed the cart out the door laden down with the stolen goods, their remaining food, and meagre belongings. Sonia lingered for a moment, looking around at the shelter that had kept them safe for near a week. It would be sealed again when they left, leaving the memory of her and Haez's passion preserved until the city finally withered away for good.

She went to the photos on the mantle and the long-dead grandparents with their eternal, frozen smiles. She let a finger graze over the human woman, with pale-blue eyes made weak from reading real flex books and smiling like she knew that lost travellers had sheltered with her.

"Thank you," she whispered to the photo before turning and following Haez outside. She shut and locked the door behind her.

Haez had opened the glider that Sonia had brought down from the upper levels. The back hatch was folded down into a ramp that he walked up and down to load in the paintings and jewellery from the chest. When the hovercart was emptied, he hit the button to make it contract back down. It had been active too long, however, and instead of neatly folding back into a little block, it groaned and crunched down into a spiny lump. Sonia picked it up with a sigh before tossing it off the walkway.

"Sorry," Haez said. Sonia waved it away and crouched to sit back on the low ramp. She pulled out the pages of flex and set them down on the flat slope.

"This is what Ottok gave me. Super-small shadow port. Transport only comes in once every few months and they don't stay on Quantrin for more than a couple days while they're making deliveries, so we have to move fast. They shouldn't have any issues with taking the old lady's stuff for payment. Hopefully."

"Any ideas if they don't?" asked Haez.

Sonia grimaced. "It's run by chiropts. You got a bag of voles?"

"Of what?"

"Nothing," said Sonia, shaking her head. It was a rude thought to have, but the spindly bat-people gave her the creeps—even more so because they were the kind that voluntarily operated out of the most foreboding part of the planet. "I guess we'll just have to hope you got enough money at the casino."

Sonia's attention was pulled by a low noise. A thrumming buzz was coming from below them and getting louder. She jumped to her feet and took a step up the back ramp of the glider, ready to seal it shut in front of her. The noise crescendoed until it sounded like a swarm of angry bees. All at once and all around them, drones burst forth from the lower levels—all different sizes with packages strapped to their undersides. Sonia looked off over the level and as far as she could see were the drones erupting up like a flock of birds. The flock thinned as they spread out in all directions, preparing to carry their bounties through the expanse of Quantrin.

She never knew drones could be so beautiful. For all the dirt and venom that ran through Quantrin's veins, there was still room for little drones that flew through the air as gracefully as humans swimming in water. Her breath trembled from the weight of the sudden rush of emotion.

"I guess the transport came in," Haez breathed, looking at the automatons swirling in all directions.

"Hey, Haez," Sonia started quietly, not looking away from the flock, "do you think we'll ever see him again?"

Haez slipped his hand around hers and gave it a gentle squeeze. "I hope so."

They stood silently and watched as the droids dispersed. Soon, all that remained were the handful that bore the heaviest burdens, bobbing and veering like bumblebees under the weight. Haez broke the silence first.

"It's time." Sonia nodded and crouched to gather the spread of flex. Haez continued, "We need to stay away from the wastes as long as we can. The radiation is going to be hell enough, even inside a shielded transport. We should be able to go straight down and then cut across."

"Sounds like you know exactly what you're doing, handsome," she replied, standing with the gathered flex, and walking to the passenger's side. As she eased herself into the seat, Haez gave a nervous laugh while moving to the driver's side.

"It's been a while since I've flown one of these. You sure you don't want to?"

Sonia gave him a teasing smile and kicked her feet up by the flexiglass viewscreen, "I couldn't possibly. I'm ever so tired, Haez. You know, I've spent the last five days stuck with some brute of a mephite? I may not recover."

He grinned and shook his head, getting into the driver's seat, "The monster. And to such a fragile young lady."

"I know, I'm a wilting bloom."

"You're a pain in my ass, is what you are."

She leaned over and gave him a kiss on the cheek, "It's a great ass."

With that, the glider hummed to life and lifted away from the platform. Haez steered it away from the residential block and dropped down between the walkways to the lower levels.

• • • • ● • ● • • • •

Hours passed as they sunk down between levels with no end in sight and no sound except the soft warbling hum of the glider. Each level was much like the one they left behind, with walkways clogged by garbage except for occasional tracks left behind by *something*. Eventually, even the garbage thinned out. Clearly there were enough levels above catching debris that even the trash stopped reaching the depths.

With the garbage out of sight and more short towers crowding in, the original vision of the city became clear. It was hard to believe coming from the chaotic sprawl of the upper levels that the foundations of the city were so stark and orderly. The Quantrin that Sonia knew had towers that rounded, twisted and tapered according to the whims of whoever oversaw the segment's construction, and all were cluttered with ladders, stairwells, and jutting signs. Here, you could tell that every building had the exact same dimensions, with identical spacing between. Each level consisted of single walkways projected from each of the four sides of each building, forming perfect stacked grids.

Whoever had laid this original groundwork for Quantrin would be horrified with what it had become, twisted organically into the image of its inhabitants—hedonistic, horrible, and alive. But as much as Sonia despised the city, she couldn't imagine living in this version of it. She felt like she was trapped between the tombstones of giants.

The light that came from the strips along the tower sides was hardly enough to see by. As they went deeper, those lights became more and more anemic before fizzling out entirely.

Then nothing. Sonia rubbed at her eyes, feeling like she was suddenly blindfolded. Her only sense of position in space was the ever-present lift in her stomach that said they were still descending.

"Haez?" She pawed in the darkness towards his seat. She jumped when his hand grabbed her own.

"I'm right here," he said, rubbing a thumb over the back of her hand. "Can you see anything?"

Sonia shook her head, breath coming faster. "Can you?"

"Not much. I think we're close to the bottom. We can stay at this height the rest of the way."

Like a jinx was spoken into the world, the glider gave an alarming shake. Haez's hand stiffened in Sonia's grip and then jerked away as he fiddled with the controls. Sonia could feel them slowing.

"What's wrong?" she asked. Haez cursed.

"Propulsion is failing. Not sure which idiot you stole this thing from, but they were not taking care of it. Hold on."

The forward motion dwindled out to nothing, and they started to sink straight down. The drop became faster and faster as Haez frantically worked the controls. At the last second, Haez flipped something that halted the drop abruptly, making Sonia's stomach lurch downward. After a second, it gently lowered to hover inches above the ground. Sonia heard him give a sigh of relief.

"We're at the bottom. It'll have to be repulsion-only. Otherwise, we're going to lose power all together. Do you have any light rods left?" Sonia nodded and reached for her satchel. Haez stopped her with a gentle hand. "Save them. You stay in the glider. I'll push."

"Oh, fuck that, I'm not staying blind down here. What if you get separated from me?" she hissed.

"Exactly. What if something happens to me and you've used them all? If you have to leave me behind to run, you can't be blind."

Sonia's gut turned to ice at the thought of what might happen to him outside the safe boundaries of the glider. "No leaving each other behind."

"We'll see. Let me see the flex." Sonia pawed around and held out the page. Haez's face was suddenly lit up by the dim glow of the glider's control panel. He held it close to the illuminated buttons to examine the scrawled notes, and then peered through the viewscreen.

"Looks like it should be that way. Maybe a day's walk," he said, nodding into the darkness. Haez folded down the door of the glider to step out.

In the distance, there was a faint grinding noise. Haez and Sonia both froze. It was only audible because of the blanket of silence. Like the grinding of a stone underfoot. Haez leaned back into the glider and flicked a switch to turn the lights off again. Then he took the gun off his belt and passed it to Sonia.

"Only use it if there's no other choice. No extra noise. No lights."

Sonia nodded back and clenched the gun in her hand. Haez moved behind the softly humming glider and, stepping as quietly as he could, started to push them forward.

· · · ● · ● · · · ·

Eventually, Sonia's eyes adjusted to the low light—at least enough that she could see the barren stone foundations that lay between each massive tower base. The narrow streets between them were eerily empty. Even if most of the garbage was picked up by the higher walkways, she at least would have expected to see a little that had slipped through the cracks from when those lower levels were still occupied. Hell, even a dead animal would have been a reassuring sight. The only way anything stayed that clean was if someone or something was cleaning it.

The only thing that might have been worse than the dark was the icy cold of a land without a speck of sunlight. Sonia shivered bitterly in the glider, wrapped in one of the blankets taken from the abandoned unit. Haez didn't complain but Sonia was sure that the physical exertion was the only thing keeping him from freezing through his coat.

As Haez pushed, she squinted into the black. Every so often, she saw something moving in the distance. Maybe just a waver of darker shadow in the black, or maybe something moving too quick for her to perceive.

"Haez," she whispered, wanting to know if he could see them better. No reply. She looked behind to where he was pushing. Even though his feet kept them moving forward, his head was slumped down between his arms, and each step was a bit shakier than the last. They didn't have much time to recover from his *bytrr*, and the hours of driving and walking had laced the exhaustion back through his body.

Sonia tied her blanket around her shoulders like a cloak and folded her glider door down a crack. She was careful not to let it scrape against the ground, instead hopping from the door to land softly on the stone. The glider kept going forward, and Sonia stepped beside Haez as it passed, putting her own hands on the back panel to help push. Haez jumped like he was woken from a spell when she appeared. He opened his mouth to say something but looked like he was dozing off standing up.

"Haez," Sonia said firmly, "get in the glider. I'm going to find somewhere for us to rest."

He shook his head but stopped pushing, leaning against the back of the glider. She saw his knees starting to buckle and jammed herself under his arm before he hit the ground.

"Come on, big guy. You did good." She practically had to carry him to the back door. Wedging Haez against the side of the vehicle and balancing on one foot, she used the other to hit the button that would drop the ramp. It folded down to the ground with a quiet click of synthsteel on stone. She walked him up the ramp and flopped his body across the back bench seat. He was asleep before the door folded shut.

After closing the passenger door as well, she returned to the back of the glider, now hyper-alert with her eyes darting uncontrollably.

Find somewhere to rest. Haez needed her.

As she pushed, she focused on the towers, trying to find one that had an entrance big enough for them and the glider. If they left it outside, it would be fair game for whatever was responsible for the clean streets.

She also wanted to avoid anything with small doors. Many of them appeared to have been forced open long ago, and the entrances were clogged with shredded materials, save for the small openings at the bottom. Dens. Insulated with all the garbage that might have once fallen like rain and reinforced with what Sonia shuddered to realize was bones. She stepped extra quietly near those doorways.

There was a glint in the darkness, almost imperceptible through the millennia of rust and frost that covered the sides of the bases. An old-style rolling door. Probably a maintenance entrance that hadn't been used since the people had left. Sonia paused the glider in front and ran her hands around the edges that she could reach. Using her fingertips, she dug into the crevasses until she found one that felt familiar. She fished the skewer out of her pocket and used the tip to carefully scrape away frost. Underneath was the telltale divot she was looking for—the emergency release. *Thanks, Dad.*

She fed the skewer down the track until it clinked against the release at end of the channel. She gave it a push. Nothing moved; it was too stiff with age. She tried again, flattening one palm against the back of the skewer, and using her other hand to strike it in like a hammer. With a grinding click, the bottom of the door popped out of its latches. The unsealed air puffed out, dusty and stinking and *warm.* Sonia gave a satisfied grin and reached under the door to roll it up.

The metal screamed. Rust on rust on frost shrieked out into the gloom. Sonia flinched and froze, looking around into the spaces between towers as the noise echoed out for miles.

The echoes died down. A new sound took their place. Distant gurgles and clicks came from all sides and slowly built to a cacophonous chatter. The shadows shifted faster and with direction—towards them.

"Oh, shit," Sonia breathed, running back behind the glider. She pushed hard and shoved it through the bay doors, letting it drift and crunch against a softly glowing interior structure. There was no time to care. She ran back to the rolling door and tried to grab hold of the bottom edge, momentum having carried it up and out of her reach. Her hand swiped a few inches too low to get a grip. The amorphous shifting had defined itself into individual shapes—quadrupedal, large enough to make her feel ill, and approaching fast.

She looked around frantically for anything that could help her reach the bottom edge of the door. The blanket. She ripped her head out of the knotted loop and tried to swing it up at the latches. It swished uselessly past. They were close enough for Sonia to hear the wet slap of feet against stone and the rustling of creatures crawling from garbage-blocked dens.

With one last attempt, she jumped as high as she could and, with a harsh yell, swung the blanket out. The knotted loop slipped over a hook latch. When it went taut, Sonia let her feet swing out and tuck in against her body, using her full weight to drag the screaming door down faster. Her back hit the ground first, and just before the door slammed and latched into place, a translucent, skeletal hand reached into view.

The sounds outside were dampened instantly. Still, enough pierced the door that she could hear the giddy clicking turn into angry chitters and hisses. The rusty metal was scratched at and thumped against but stayed solid. Sonia let out a shaky breath of relief.

They were safe. Trapped, but safe.

It was easier to see in the tower base than outside. This bottom layer wasn't divided into units like the upper levels, instead forming a massive empty space peppered throughout with support pillars, the tower's conduit running through the centre. The insulation had been eaten by time and left the dangerously hot column exposed, wobbling the air with ambient heat and glowing a soft red in the dark. The glider had a smoking scorch-mark where it had impacted and drifted away.

Sonia peered into the glider. Haez was still sleeping. In the soft, red warmth, he looked healthier and more peaceful than she had ever seen him. *Not that it counts for much, given what we've been through,* she thought. She reached into the glider and lowered the seat backs as carefully as she could, trying not to wake him. He didn't stir as the seats shifted—if Sonia didn't know better, she would have thought he was dead. When the back bench had been turned into a wide platform, she crawled into the glider and curled against his side. They still had a day. She burrowed closer against him and willed his strong, warm body to soothe her into a dreamless sleep.

But it didn't. While Haez rested, Sonia lay awake listening to the sound of skeletal fingers clawing the edge of the door and imagining wet footsteps lurking in the shadows.

15

Haez

Haez was warm. The edge between sleep and waking was brushing his consciousness and the cloying heat was keeping him from reaching it. Then he remembered: He should be cold. He should be walking. He should be saving Sonia.

Sonia.

The thought woke him in a panic, limbs trying to flail him upright. His sudden movement slipped his body off the edge of the platform and down into the dirty space behind the front seats. Once his mind caught up to where he was, he groaned and tried to push himself back up, even as his horn snagged on the material covering the bench. Sonia's head popped up from outside the glider and looked through the open door at him.

"Are you okay?" she asked. He rolled himself back up to lay across the seats and gave a grumbled acknowledgement. She ducked back down under the glider. Whatever she was doing was making the vehicle rock back and forth in a way that threatened to lull Haez back to sleep. He forced himself to sit up again and slid down to let his feet rest on the lowered ramp.

"Where are we?" he asked, looking around the tower interior. Sonia looked up again, illuminated by one of her sparked light rods on the ground and the glow of the dangerously hot pillar in the middle of the room.

"Inside a tower base. You were out for a few hours. We should still have time, but there's another problem," Sonia said, gesturing at the rolling door set in the wall behind Haez.

"Is it broken?"

"No. Just noisy. Everything in earshot knows that we're in here."

Haez cocked his head and listened before shrugging. "I don't hear anything. They might have gotten bored and ran off."

Sonia's face gave a paranoid twitch. "I don't know. We don't know how smart these things are. They might be trying to trick us into coming out."

Her eyes were manic and underscored by deep purple circles, and the more she spoke, the quicker and more irritable her voice became. Haez may have slept, but she clearly had not. Looking down at where she worked, he carefully asked, "What are you doing?"

She gave an unhinged smile as she looked up from the loose wires she had pulled from the glider. "I can fix the propulsion. We'll never get past those things on foot. It might not have much power, but we're close! We could get there in ten minutes! I'll drive and you can shoot!"

He looked at her and then looked away. She was in no state to do anything, let alone drive through a swarm of monsters. Not unless he did something to make it a lot easier for her.

"Going through them is crazy, Sonia. Now, I can see if there's a side exit. I can lure them away and then you—"

"Stop doing that!" she screamed at him suddenly. He jumped and looked at her in confusion.

"Doing what?"

"Trying to find an excuse for me to leave you and for you to get yourself killed! You keep doing it! And I fucking hate it!"

"Sonia, I'm just—"

"Just what?" she continued, "Trying to find some excuse to get away from me? Am I that horrible to be around?"

Hearing those words made him burn with sadness. How could she possibly think that? He wanted to find every person who had ever made her feel that way and make them pay for their stupidity. He met her wild stare steadily and said, "I want to stay around you more than I want to keep breathing. If I have to stop breathing for you to be safe, I will—and gladly."

"Bullshit," she said, jabbing an accusing finger at him. "You want to know what I think? I think you're just so scared of fucking up again that you'd rather die before you got the chance."

"Hey—" he started warningly, but she ploughed on, her sleep-starved face becoming wilder with every word.

"No, I'm right. And I know I'm right. I don't care that you're a fuckup, Haez. So am I. And I want to go with you to your forest world and sleep for ten years and not feel scared and alone for once. If you abandon me too, you don't get to be a perfect, shining memory. I'll curse you out every fucking day and I'll curse myself out for ever loving you."

Her words hung in the silence between them. It took a moment before Sonia realized what she'd said. Her face closed off and she turned back to the mess of wires hanging out of the glider. They sat in silence for a minute before Haez stepped down the ramp and lowered himself to the ground. He sat behind Sonia with his long legs splayed out on either side, pulled her back to his chest, and rested his chin on top of her head. The wires lay limp in her hands as she took in the warmth of his body against hers. They stayed silent like that for a few minutes before he spoke again.

"You're right. I am scared," he said quietly. "I'm terrified. Everything bad that's happened since we met has been my fault. I'm why we missed the first transport. I'm why you had to go to Ottok. I'm why we got into this mess in the first place. The only good thing in all of this is you. And I feel like it's only a matter of time before I mess up again and you get taken away too."

His grip around her tightened crushingly. "I can't take it. Not just the thought of you getting hurt. The thought that eventually I'll screw things up so bad that you'll look at me the same way everyone else does. Like I'm worthless."

Sonia twisted in his embrace to face him, lifting to her knees, and resting both her palms on the sides of his face. "You're not worthless."

"And you aren't alone. I'm yours, Sonia. I've been yours since you walked into that bar."

Her bottom lip trembled, and her tired eyes took on a shine. Still, she pinned him with a demanding stare. "Not if you're dead. Promise me you'll drop the sacrificial thinking. Promise me you'll live."

"I promise," he breathed, the air from that vow filling the space between them. Haez gently wrapped a hand around the back of her neck and pulled her into a tender kiss. Sonia returned it, the soft brushes of lips undercut by her hands clutching desperately around the collar of his coat. When they parted, they pressed their foreheads together and shared each other's breath.

The quiet moment was broken by a little giggle from Sonia. Haez smiled and asked, "What?"

"Since the bar? Even with that cheap-ass wig?"

"Especially with the cheap-ass wig. I love a flammable-looking woman."

The tears she had held back made her laughter bubbly. She leaned in for another kiss, muttering, "Fucking jackass," against his lips.

When they finally separated, Haez said, "Well, if we're getting out of here together, I guess you'd better get this thing fixed up. Your jackass is driving, though."

· · · ● · ● · · ·

It took close to an hour before Sonia was able to get the right wires connected to each other. Haez sat in the driver's seat and tried the controls after each of her attempts. She rolled out from under the glider again and crouched beside it, staring daggers at the uncooperative scrap heap.

"Try again," she shouted to Haez, not breaking her glare.

He flipped the controls, and it finally gave a flatulent sputter and drifted forward. Sonia jumped up from the ground, clapping and giving a triumphant bark of laughter.

"Oooooh what did I say? Am I good or am I good?" she said, doing a celebratory shuffle. Haez smirked at her display and obligingly clapped.

"Never doubted you, pretty lady. We ready to do this?"

She faltered, like she had forgotten why she had been fixing the glider in the first place. Then she started nodding absently.

"Yeah, yeah, yeah. Yeah, I'm good."

Haez steered the glider until it sat with its nose an inch from the rolling door. Sonia went to the side of the door with her skewer in hand. Her hand grazed over the wall until she found the depression of the emergency release. She used the implement to scratch away some debris and threaded the skewer down the channel. When it clicked into place at the end of the hole, she faced Haez and gave him a nod. He reached across the glider and let down the passenger door before nodding back.

Sonia took one last deep breath. Then she moved fast. With a quick smack to the back of her hand, her palm pushed the skewer into the release mechanism. The door unlatched quietly, but she still ran to fling it open from the bottom as fast as possible. Anything could have been silently watching. It was still screaming its ascent up the rusty tracks when she jumped over the door ramp into the passenger's side, yelling, "Go, go, go!"

Sonia was barely able to get the passenger's door folded up before Haez slammed on the speed and sent the glider ripping out of the tower like a shot. The slapdash repairs were already threatening to fail, with an alarming clunking sound coming from the engine. Sonia's fears had been warranted though, and pale shapes were already running from the shadows. He didn't dare slow.

"Which way?" he yelled at her over the engine noise. When she didn't respond, he glanced over and wanted to smack himself. The time spent inside the heat-lit room had ruined any adjustments her vision made to the darkness. She was blind again, looking around with bugged-out eyes trying to catch the slightest slivers of light.

And I almost made her go alone. You worthless idiot, he thought.

"Um, right, I think?" she yelled back at him, squinting out into the black. Once they cleared the tower block, Haez pulled a hard right, letting the warbling glider drift across the lane. They were at least outstripping the main pack of creatures, but the horde was growing, being fed new monsters from the garbage-insulated dens that lined the streets.

"Get a light rod," he shouted. "You need to guide me!"

Sonia nodded frantically in the dark and grabbed her satchel. She had to set the gun aside to dig around blindly until she produced one of the precious rods. When she ripped the ignition strip out of the core, the light was sparked.

One of the pale creatures leapt from the shadows toward the glider.

It landed above them with a thump and started clawing at the roof and doors. Sonia screamed and reached for the gun. Scrunching her eyes shut, she fired a shot into the roof. It missed. The creature dug its bony fingers into the seam around her door. Sonia lined up another shot as the door popped down, dragging against the stone with a shriek and shredding from its hinges.

This time when she shot, the monster yelped and rolled off the back of the roof. For a moment, everything was silent except for the whir of the glider. Sonia let out a sigh of relief and turned the light rod to the folio of flex.

"Take a left, another right, and then stay straight. We should be there in five minutes," she said. Haez slid into the turns and accelerated down their straight shot to freedom.

The clunking sound from the bottom of the glider continued. Then grew louder.

And then stopped. With a crack, part of the machine work of the vehicle broke off and disappeared into the shadowed streets behind.

The glider gave a groan of protest and slowed. Sonia looked down in a panic and slammed her palms against the dashboard.

"No, no, no, you bastard! I fixed you!"

"Fix it better!" Haez shouted. Sonia dove onto the controls in the cab. As they slowed, the creatures started to gain on them.

Sonia fiddled with the power balancers, making the glider lurch and wobble dangerously. Haez's eyes darted between her and the road. In the distance was the small amber glow of the port.

"What in the hells are you doing?" Haez yelled at her. She shot him an apologetic look.

"You trust me, right?"

"Why—"

Before he could ask, Sonia flipped one of the switches. The back of the glider dropped and dragged against the ground, sending up a shower of sparks from the screeching metal. Her hands moved fast on the control panel, and a moment later, the power drawn from the repulsors poured into the propulsion system. They shot forward again, still trailing the cascade of sparks that marked them with a beacon in the black.

The distant glow grew closer and so did the creatures. The noise and light painted them as a target and even more of the greedy monsters emerged from their hiding spots.

Haez kept his eyes trained on their destination. So close.

The glider jerked hard to the side as a screaming weight jumped against Haez's door. Sonia tried to grab the top of the door frame, but her hand slipped on the blood left behind by the first creature. Haez watched the moment stretch into eternity as his world went tumbling out of the side of the glider.

"Sonia!" he screamed, twisting around to see her rolling to a stop as the glider left her behind. Without thinking, he slammed the brakes and wrenched the controls into a sharp turn. The strain was too much for the glider. As he turned, the engines groaned and gave out, dropping the front down with a crash and sending the whole thing skidding sideways before crunching to a stop. He barely waited for it to still before he bolted out of his door and sprinted back to where Sonia was stumbling to her feet. Descending upon her was the roiling, pale mass of creatures. One of her ankles was bent at an angle and reduced her run to a limping shamble. She was too slow. He screamed at his muscles to move faster.

Suddenly, there was a screech and thump and one of the creatures jumped in Haez's path, blocking Sonia from his view. It was the first one that was still enough for him to truly see.

It might have been a person once, a thousand generations ago before the pragmatic hand of evolution and an endless wash of radiation guided it into what faced him now. Its limbs were thin and sinuous, stretched over with glossy pale skin that rippled disgustingly in the light as it began to circle him.

The worst part was the face, or what remained of one. The skin was thinner over its skull, showing all the veins tracing over jutting bones and through the membrane of skin that covered its empty eye sockets. Still, it watched him, sniffing quickly through its nose when it moved to pounce.

There was a scream of rage as Sonia was suddenly there, latching onto the thing's back. In her hand was Ottok's skewer, which she stabbed down into the space between its neck and shoulder. It squealed in pain and tried to throw her off, but she tightened her limbs around it and brought the skewer down over and over again.

She didn't stop screaming as its neck was reduced to shredded pulp. Finally, she jammed the skewer as deep as it would go and left it embedded in the creature as it dropped. She stood over it, face crazed and splattered with blood, and screamed at it once more for good measure. When she looked up at Haez, her eyes went out of focus and she swayed in place, her blind rage overtaken by the bone-on-bone grinding in her ankle. Haez leapt forward and caught her in his arms before she fainted.

We're getting out of this together, he repeated in his head like a prayer as he hefted her up and ran towards the port.

Behind them, the creatures slowed at the corpse, wasting no time in ripping it to pieces and sending blood and gristle spraying into the air. They swarmed over it like a mass of ants, and when the crush cleared, it was with many of the creatures scattering out to the spaces between towers. Each dragged bits of remaining bone or tendon to add to their dens. The street bore no sign of the mangled body. Those that captured no prize from the feeding frenzy focused again on the living prey.

Haez could hear them close at his heels, their hands and feet slapping wetly against the ground as they chased them down. He didn't dare turn to see how close they were, instead focusing on Sonia as she fought to stay conscious and on how close they were to salvation. The first soft glow of sunlight peeked over the flattened towers of the wastes.

"Help us!" Haez screamed, his voice sizzling from exhaustion. "Passengers! Help!"

His voice was so shredded that it was drowned out by the creatures' wet clicks. He tried again. "Please! We can pay!" Damp breath steamed against the back of his thighs.

From the port, a little glowing spot shot up into the air. It hovered for a second before exploding into blinding white light.

Sonia and Haez flinched back and covered their eyes, but the creatures screamed in agony. The light sizzled at their membranous skin and left angry, blackened blisters behind. They turned and fled from the port lest they be burnt again.

Haez slowed his run and turned so they could watch the creatures retreat back between the buildings. He laughed incredulously. Sonia couldn't manage a laugh, but she turned her head to watch them go as tears of relief streamed down her face.

Haez carefully lowered her to the ground, and they clung to each other, laughing, crying, and shaking.

"I thought I lost you," he whispered to Sonia, voice thick with emotion. She shook her head, her hands clenching around his shoulders like he could vanish at any second.

"You're not getting rid of me that easy," she replied. He smiled against her mouth and peppered her with kisses.

"Never," he said, "We're going to Ghusn and we're going to sleep for ten years and every night I'm going to eat that sweet pu—"

"You scumbags."

The deadly calm voice cut through their relief and sent ice through Haez's veins. They both looked towards the entrance to the port.

Staukar. He stood on the platform leading to the port silhouetted by the dawning light and flanked on either side by the Delnul brothers. Rakir held his gun threateningly at his side while saying something to one of the chiropt spacers. The chiropt raised its spidery hands placatingly and backed away to retreat behind a mess of crates. Proll had his gun trained on them but kept looking from them to Staukar, unease written on his face. Three of Staukar's other goons leaned back against shipping containers, binders and ropes in hand.

Staukar gave them a look down his nose like a dog had shit in his path.

"I've been looking for you."

16

Haez

Haez lifted himself from the ground and reached down to help Sonia to her feet, never turning his gaze from Staukar and his men. He tried to move his body between her and the gun barrels, but she hobbled out to stand shoulder-to-elbow.

"None of that bullshit," she said quietly. He gave her a small smile and slid his hand over hers. The slight tremor in her fingers was the only sign of her fear. *What a woman*, he found himself thinking again.

"I love you," he said under his breath.

She smiled back and echoed in a whisper, "I love you." They turned to face Staukar. His mouth spread into a smile that didn't touch his cold eyes.

"Isn't that touching," he said, turning his attention fully to Haez. "You're a difficult man to track down, Haez. Have you been avoiding me? That hurts. I know new love is a whirlwind, but that's no excuse for bad manners."

"We can still talk about this—" Haez started, but was cut off by Staukar pressing a finger to his lips and making a shushing sound. He then turned his gaze on Sonia.

"And you," he said, letting his eyes roam over Sonia's body, "you must be Sonia Jentis." The way he said her name like he was tasting it made Haez's hackles rise. He focused on Sonia's hand in his own, tightening her grip and anchoring him in place lest his rage drive him to recklessness. Staukar continued, "You're a little broad for my tastes, but I can think of some clients who would pay handsomely for a few hours of your company. I see why Ottok wanted to keep you a secret."

A breath caught in Sonia's throat at Ottok's name, and she blurted out, "What did you do to him? Is he okay?"

"Worry about yourself, little girl," Staukar said coldly.

Haez interjected to try to get his focus off Sonia.

"Everything is in the glider, Staukar," he said, gesturing back at where he left the broken-down vehicle. "Just take it back. We'll leave the planet. You'll never have to see us again."

"Everything, Haez?" Staukar asked, raising an eyebrow.

"You already got the bracelet back from the litto. So yes, everything." Sonia looked at him sideways, but kept her mouth shut about the lie.

Staukar sighed and reached into his jacket, feeling around in the deep pocket. "This is a problem, Haez. Every time I want to trust you, you keep letting me down. Always with the lies."

"It's not. Check the glider if you don't believe me."

Staukar pulled what he was feeling for out of his coat He smirked at Sonia before tossing a fist-sized bundle off the platform to roll to their feet.

"A little birdy told me differently."

Bile rose in Haez's throat as he realized what had been thrown out. Sonia dropped to her knees and unwrapped the bundle with shaking hands, revealing the pale yellow of a familiar pierced beak. It was splintered and cracked along the stress-lines of a lifetime of drilling, but the hoop through the bridge was intact. The back edge was tinged red and still bore feathers and torn skin. Sonia couldn't keep her disgust and horror down. She hastily covered it again and pushed it away before turning and vomiting onto the ground, letting out anguished moans in between heaves.

The enforcers that had been hanging back laughed uproariously at Sonia's reaction. Haez never wanted to frighten her again the way he had at *The Celeste*, but looking at Staukar's pleased face and the way he chuckled so freely at her pain, he longed for nothing more than to take the crime lord's skull to the stone and see how long it took to make it split.

"He held out for a long time," Staukar said, face mockingly sombre. "He sure cared about you, Sonia. Spent a lot of his breath begging for us to let you go. But we got through to him." He paused for a moment and crouched at the edge of the platform, smirking and staring at Sonia. "Your daddy had a lovely singing voice."

As Staukar spoke, Haez stared accusingly at Rakir and Proll. The others that Staukar had brought were humans, probably the newly arrived children of his Ozarlan friends. They had no connection or loyalty to Quantrin. But the Delnuls knew Ottok—both of them having only survived until adulthood due to his care. Proll looked nearly as sick as Sonia, and Rakir—though he was better at concealing his emotions, had a dissociated glaze in his eyes. Did they watch? Was it one of them who took a bludgeon to Ottok's face until it broke?

No, Haez decided. But they knew and let it happen. Proll's words repeated in his head: *We become what we have to.*

You became cowards, Haez thought, feeling like his blood had been replaced with pure, liquid hatred.

Staukar finally grew bored of Sonia's sobbing, now silent and muffled into her hands. He straightened, turned away, and breezily said to Proll, "Stun them."

Proll took aim with his gun. And faltered. His eyes darted between them and Staukar until he forced out, "Do we need to do this, boss?" Haez could practically hear the bones in Staukar's neck clicking mechanically as he swiveled his head to look at Proll.

"What?"

"I only thought—"

With a twitch of his hand, something in Staukar's palm popped open to form a baton. He walloped it across Proll's jaw, making him cry out and drop to one knee. Even Rakir couldn't stay totally impassive, body going stiff and face flushing an angry purple. He looked on as Staukar, with his face suddenly enraged, leaned in an inch from his brother's face and grabbed one of his horns to force his head still.

"I'm paying you. That means you do what I tell you. I tell you to shoot your brother, you do it. I tell you to shove that gun up your ass and turn yourself into a firecracker, then you fucking do it. And if I tell you that I want you to stun both of these dirtbags so I can take them home and let my boys kill them nice and slow . . . " he trailed off, staring at Proll with wild eyes.

Proll looked away from Staukar with a mouthful of blood and shoulders rounded with resignation. He sputtered, "I-I do it." Staukar gave him a sharkish grin as he nodded and stepped back, gesturing again at the pair.

"Actually," Staukar started again, reaching out to Proll's gun. He flicked a switch and it whirred in anticipation. "If you feel squeamish about stunning, why don't you just pop their little kneecaps out for me? This can be an important lesson in not making me repeat myself."

Haez looked back and forth between Proll, taking up his gun again, and Rakir, who was probably close to cracking a molar with how tightly his jaw was clenched. A stupid, stupid idea came to him.

"You gonna take that, Rakir?" he called out. "I'd never let anyone talk to my brother that way."

Rakir shot him a glare, straightened his posture more and crossed his gun across his chest, the picture of a professional mercenary. From where Sonia sat on the ground, she balled a hand in Haez's pant leg and looked up at him, a silent question on her tear-streaked face. Internally, he begged her to trust him one last time.

Survive this, you cowardly pricks.

"I know I pissed you off," he continued, "I know you were trying to get back at me when you told me about the job. But you don't have to be treated like this."

Rakir's face went ashen. Staukar's baton creaked in his grip as he turned his attention to Rakir. Staukar was silent for a long time before Rakir finally spoke.

"You're not buying this, right, Boss?" he said, voice overly dismissive.

"It's funny," Staukar said with deadly calm. "Not many people know about my family home. You were on bodyguard detail for my mother last rotation, weren't you. And then Haez just happens to mark the wrong house."

"He's lying. Just like he lies about everything else."

Staukar's eyes burned with murderous intent when he replied, "No, he's not."

"Staukar—"

"BOYS," he screamed at the three other men who jumped to attention. "KILL THEM. ALL OF THEM!"

Before the other men could fumble their guns off their belts, there was a zinging sound and Staukar hit the ground with a sizzling hole through his head. Proll froze where he stood for a moment, gun still whirring in his hands. With wide, horrified eyes, he looked at his brother, who couldn't hide his shock. Rakir's eyes deadened, and with sharp accuracy, he wheeled around and fired three shots of his own, one for each of Staukar's remaining men. They all hit the ground within seconds.

Then he swung around to aim at Haez and Sonia. Haez flinched back, ready for the final blast. Sonia grabbed the bottom of his coat, yanked him down to the ground, and threw her arms wide to block his body.

"Just let us leave the planet!" she begged Rakir, voice watery and hoarse. "We'll never come back; we'll never tell anyone what happened!"

"We can't risk that," Rakir replied, his voice forced flat but the pinch of his brows betraying his distress at Sonia's earnest plea. Proll approached him and leaned in.

"Come on," he muttered to his brother. "They're leaving any-ways." Rakir's shoulders rounded when he looked to Proll, his mask dropping enough to bleed anxiety into his pained expression.

"One witness, Proll. That's all it takes. We get rid of them and tell Vrix that Haez got Staukar and the others before we put them down. Vrix takes over and we stay in a job. If anyone even got wind that these two were still alive—"

"They won't!" shouted Sonia. Rakir raised his gun at her, but Proll put a hand on it and pushed it down to point at the ground.

"There's some stuff you can't come back from, Rakir."

Rakir fixed his brother with a desperate stare but after a moment, he sighed and lowered his gun. After wearily rubbing a hand over his eyes, he jerked his head towards the port landing pad. "What about the dock workers?"

"You need not worry about us," came a wispy voice from a shadowed corner. The brothers jumped, Rakir swinging his gun around to point at the noise. One of the chiropts was unfolding her arms from around her pencil-thin form as she stepped into the light. The webbing that stretched the length of her body from wrist to ankle stirred her open-sided poncho. She bared her fangs and crinkled her glassy red eyes in an attempt at a smile.

"Apologies for eavesdropping. We so rarely have such excitement during our stop overs," she said as she hunched over the scattered bodies and chittered excitedly like a child at the zoo.

"How do we know you won't tell anyone what happened here?" Rakir asked, not lowering his gun. The chiropt paused in stroking her hyperextended fingers over Staukar's unmoving face and looked at Rakir like she forgot he was there. She straightened and folded her fingers in front of her chest.

"Attention is bad for our business. I'm not sure how any of you found our location, but it is nothing but trouble." The chiropt trilled irritably before continuing, "We will have to find a new landing area before we can continue business on Quantrin. All trouble, all trouble."

"We need transport. Please. What will it cost for the two of us?" Sonia asked the chiropt, still eyeing Rakir suspiciously. The chiropt twitched her fingers and summoned two fat, hovering drones from the loading dock. They buzzed out to the glider and towed it towards the port. When it bumped gently against the platform, the chiropt bent sharply at the waist to examine the contents. She chittered thoughtfully before looking up to them, the same grimace of a smile on her face.

"All of it."

Weakly, Sonia protested, "That's too much—"

"Done," Haez interrupted. He squeezed a reassuring hand on her shoulder and rose to his feet. He yelled to Rakir, "What do you say? We leave Quantrin and don't look back. If anyone asks, we died after killing Staukar and the others. We can all walk away from this."

Rakir and Proll shared a look before Rakir nodded and finally holstered his gun. The chiropt raised one of her hands. "If I may make a request: would you please leave the bodies?" She didn't elaborate; Haez didn't want to know.

Rakir cut in, saying, "We need Staukar. I don't care what you do with the others, but it'll be more suspicious if we don't bring him back."

The chiropt huffed but chittered her agreement. She turned back to Haez and Sonia. "We will leave shortly. Our drones will attend to your payment."

With that, she turned and glided away, going back towards the transport. A flock of the rotund drones buzzed to the glider and started taking individual items to the loading dock.

Haez turned back to Sonia and reached down to help her up from the ground. Before taking his hand, she reached for the handker-chief-wrapped bundle and clutched it to her chest, careful not to let any of the beak peek out from the fabric. He then pulled her up and gently scooped her into his arms. She slumped against his chest, still holding what remained of Ottok over her heart.

With Sonia cradled to him, he slowly walked up the ramp leading to the platform. All the aches and bruising had caught up to him and it took all he had to stay strong and sturdy for Sonia, just a little longer. They passed Proll first, whose eyes were cast downward with shame. He murmured a hoarse apology to Sonia as they walked by. She didn't respond, but the icy contempt on her face said she had heard and would not spare a shred of forgiveness. Haez was right there with her.

Then they came to Rakir. He was crouched over Staukar's body, rifling through his pockets. When they approached, he stood with something in hand.

"Let me see your wrist," he said flatly. Haez didn't stop glaring at him, but shifted Sonia so Rakir could see the hand that braced her back. He tapped the object to the bracelet and after a moment, it broke apart—not along some hidden clasp, but with every scale joint that formed it separating, like the tendons holding it together had suddenly vanished. They fell to the platform with a delicate tinkling sound.

"There," he said. "You're free. Get out of here."

Haez let the silence sit for a moment before asking, "Is that all you have to say?"

Rakir's face contorted like he wanted to cry but had long since forgotten how. "What do you want me to say? If words could undo any of this, I'd say them all. But they won't. Ottok is gone. And I have to live with that."

"Good," Haez snarled. "Live with it every fucking day of your miserable life. I hope you never leave this planet. You deserve each other."

Haez stalked away, leaving the Delnuls behind to mop up the mess. He wove through the packages that still needed to be loaded and carried Sonia up the ramp to the massive transport. Inside, another chiropt monitored the drones from a datapad. He absently pointed them down a corridor without a word. Sleeping quarters.

Haez peeked inside a handful until he found one without signs of another occupant. It wasn't much more than a closet with a single narrow bunk and a side-table, but it was only a few days' travel to Ghusn. It would do. He sat down on the edge of the bed and gently eased the bundle out of Sonia's hands to set aside. Then he shifted them both onto the bunk and leaned back against the wall, Sonia still clinging to his chest.

Set in the wall to their left was a small viewport that looked out over the wastes. He had never seen them this close and maybe it was just the promise of home so near at hand, but the jagged field of ruins reminded him of looking over the top of the forest canopy.

The rising light streamed from the open sky over the wastes and illuminated his face enough to see his reflection in the flexiglass circle. It was a stranger's face, skin and horns marked permanently with the evidence of the past couple weeks. He didn't want to look into his own tired, suddenly aged eyes. Instead, he focused beyond his reflection and out over the wastes, getting brighter with each passing second. He pressed a kiss to Sonia's temple.

"Look, love," he said. "The sun's coming up."

Epilogue
Sonia

Sonia woke slowly and lazily, a cool, damp breeze stroking across her face and trying to lull her back to sleep. Her face was half-pressed into the luxuriously soft bed and crisp white sheets when she finally opened her eyes. Haez slept on beside her, mouth lolling open.

Something about this morning felt different, and it took her a minute to realize what. It was the first time in the weeks since their escape from Quantrin that she'd woken naturally with the daylight, rather than being jolted awake by another nightmare. The first time she'd woken and Haez was able to sleep on instead of rubbing her back and whispering reassurances that they were safe. It wasn't much, but it at least meant her mind was starting to heal.

Looking at his peaceful, sleeping face had her stirring in a way that she hadn't since Haez's *bytrr* and it gave her a wicked notion. Carefully, she lifted the covers and shimmied her body down until she was level with his sleep pants. She loosened them just enough for her to push them down and release his cock, sleep already making it half hard. When he didn't stir, she flicked her tongue out and traced around the rim of his broad head. He gave a sleepy moan and stiffened more against her mouth, still not waking. She smiled and lavished his length with soft licks, sucks, and strokes as she coaxed him fully to hardness.

Above the covers, she heard him breathe, "Good morning to you too" as he arched his hips towards her face. She saw the blanket crumple in his grasp, and before he could pull it away, she took as much of him as she could down her throat, struggling not to gag on the thick intrusion. When the blanket was lifted, he let out a strangled groan at the sight of her swallowing him down. She pulled off slowly, licking her lips and smiling.

"Good morning, love," she whispered. "Think you can be quiet?"

She lurched to the side as Haez rolled her onto her back, sinking into the pillowy mattress. He leaned in and his chest pushed her deeper into the bed as he kissed her ravenously.

"Can you?" he breathed against her mouth. She nodded and arched her head back to let him ravish her throat. His hands slid up her legs, pushing her sleep shirt up to bunch around her waist. She put her hand over her own mouth to muffle the weak whimper that snuck out when he slid the head of his cock through her slick to tease her clit.

Sonia quivered under him as he stroked himself against her, bringing her closer to the edge. Finally, she whined, "Haez, *please.*"

He straightened, guided himself down and with a slow push, slid into her. She bit down hard on her knuckle to stifle her noises, but the drag of his head inside her still forced out a breathy, "Oh, fuck." It wasn't as punishingly large as it had been during his *bytrr,* for which she was thankful. She didn't think she could handle that regularly without the aid of the mind-scrambling pheromones, and even now, he was stretching her to her limits.

Haez's hand moved to rub his thumb over her clit. He rocked into her gentle and deep, letting his thumb push her over the edge again and again. Each time, she tremored around him and became more boneless, lost in her own pleasure.

Finally, the gentle rocking took Haez too close to his end. He gripped her hips in both hands and gave a few more hard thrusts before tensing and rocking over her, biting his lip to hold back his own pleasured moans. Once he stopped pulsing and releasing inside her, he fell forward and caged her in his arms, nose pressed into the crook of her neck.

The sleepy morning air hung still around them. Suddenly, it was broken by a sharp knocking at the door.

"Haez, sweetie, do you think you and your girlfriend can wait until we're out of the house next time?" There was a stifled giggle of a second voice not far behind.

Sonia flushed almost as red as Haez and buried her face in the mattress in mortification. Haez tried to hold back laughter at her reaction and his own embarrassment. "Sorry, Mom," he called back to the door.

· · · · · ● · ● · · · ·

They came down the stairs from their room together, Haez leading and Sonia trailing behind, nervously adjusting her shirt. Two older mephite women moved around the small kitchen, looking out over the bright treetop city.

It was all interconnecting pathways like Quantrin, but not the chaotic sprawl of synthsteel platforms with loose railings and rusting holes. The trees flowed together organically, with each of the walkways between made by guiding branches to weave and grow together over hundreds of years. The resulting bridges were sturdier and safer than anything made of metal. The walkways that wrapped around each tree were solid ledges carved into the thick bark of each of the behemoths.

The designs of the homes echoed the outside, with everything built compactly and wrapped against the sides of the trees, blending naturally into their shapes. Inside, the home was built small across several stories adjoined by narrow stairwells. Everywhere Sonia walked inside, she wanted to let her hand run along the curved interior walls.

She could tell that whoever had first designed Quantrin must have taken their inspiration either from Ghusn or other planets like it. But they missed the point when they'd transfigured it into synthsteel and flexiglass and let it grow too high above its natural foundations. On Ghusn, you could still see the ground—and more importantly, the sky.

Not Ghusn, she reminded herself. Riluuk was the city. It had been a long time since the planet and the city were not one and the same. Haez's mothers had been quick to remind her every time she mixed it up, always with a derisive comment about Quantrin and its overdevelopment.

The women bickered playfully, one of them nearly as tall as Haez, willowy as a sapling and ashy-blue. She wore a long head wrap that ran between her slim horns and down her back, just adding to the impression of her always seeming to be swaying gracefully in the breeze. The other was short for a mephite, only slightly taller than Sonia, and built thickly like a boxer past their prime. Her head was bare, the burgundy of her scalp only interrupted by a pair of stubby, sharpened horns. She playfully snatched a bit of fruit off the breakfast platter her wife was arranging.

They both turned to the stairs at the sound of Haez and Sonia coming down. The shorter one leaned against the counter, smirking at the pair.

"Good morning, lovebirds. Have a good sleep?"

"Good morning, Ma," Haez sighed back. The tall one gave Haez an apologetic look as he moved to give her a kiss on the cheek. Sonia waved sheepishly to them both.

"Sorry about that, Mrs. Coubik—"

"I've told you, honey, Boli is fine," she replied with a smile. "Genn wanted me to scare you two, but it seemed a little mean to me."

Genn paused in sipping her syrupy purple drink and narrowed her eyes at Boli. "Snitch."

Boli leaned down to give her a kiss before straining to lift the massive platter. Genn reached in and hefted it with one hand to carry to the table.

"Breakfast, kiddos. Dig in."

· · · ● · ● · ● · · ·

"And you really watch this old stuff? Like, for pleasure?"

"Hang on, this is a good part," Sonia said, attention pulling from her food to watch the holodrama raptly. Genn sat with her on the thickly cushioned bench that flowed seamlessly into the floor. She used a long-handled eating hook to pluck food up from the plate balanced on her lap. Behind them, Haez and Boli sat at the dining table, talking quietly. Without realizing, Sonia was mouthing along the lines of the down-and-out detective on screen, twitching her face into minute expressions to match. Old habits die hard.

When the character finished their monologue, Sonia smiled and gestured at the screen, turning to Genn with an expectant look. All she got back was a blank shrug.

"Really? That doesn't just hit you in the gut?"

Genn gave her an apologetic smile and said, "Sorry, I never really got into these human shows. I don't get why they can't just say what they mean."

Haez called from the table, "You're in for it now, Ma." Sonia, who had been taking a deep breath to fuel a long tangent, paused and exhaled.

"No, it's fine. I know it's not for everyone," she said awkwardly. Boli narrowed her eyes at Haez and knocked the back of his knuckles with her own hook. He jerked his hand back and shot her a confused look but withered under her scolding glare.

"Sorry, love," he said to Sonia, standing and leaning over the back of the bench to kiss the top of her head. "I was just teasing. I like hearing you talk about it."

Sonia rubbed at one of his hands that had come down to clasp her shoulders and looked up at him with a soft smile. Genn looked back to Boli and jerked her head slightly towards the couple. Boli paused in the middle of sipping her beanta and cleared her throat.

"We were thinking about that too, Sonia. It's not quite the same as what you'd be used to, but, well, if you missed performing, we—well *Genn* really—" Boli rambled, tripping over words in her excitement.

"There's a community theatre group in the neighbourhood," Genn cut in, sharing a hopeful glance with her wife. "It's mostly mephites, but I think there's a couple other humans."

Boli nodded emphatically and jumped back in, "Yes, there's...Lio, I think? I'm sure there's more. The point is you wouldn't be the only one! Oh, they're very friendly, very welcoming. It's not going to be the same as whatever they have on *Quantrin*," she said, putting venomous emphasis on the name, like speaking it might summon it outside the window, "But Riluuk has a fine theatre community too!"

They had been like this since Haez and Sonia had arrived on Ghusn. Once the mothers had gotten over the initial shock and glee of suddenly having their son knocking at their door after years off-planet, they had focused their energy on making sure he didn't leave again. No matter how much Haez reassured them that they wouldn't be going back to Quantrin, every day they brought up some new thing that would maybe encourage them to lay down roots. Now they were trying to work on Sonia: Haez's actress girlfriend.

It wasn't a lie, not really. But there was only so much truth they could share from their lives on Quantrin without opening the floodgates of why they had to leave. And Boli and Genn didn't need the anguish of knowing what their son had suffered through without their knowledge. Instead, they got to meet Sonia, the moderately successful stage actress who Haez had met at a bar near the theatre after a show—they had been seeing each other for a little over a cycle now. She wasn't well-known enough that there was any chance that the women would try to brag about meeting her but was established enough that they wouldn't question how she actually made her money.

It wasn't a lie, but it wasn't the truth, either. Based on the worried looks that Boli had cast on Haez's broken horn and missing tooth, they probably knew more than they were letting on, but would believe whatever truth kept their son from disappearing again. Sonia could understand that. She had a feeling that she wasn't the only one in the house who'd been woken by nightmares of finding Haez's broken and lifeless body—or worse, not finding him at all.

Sonia smiled to them and looked back up to Haez, "I'll have to think about it. We're going to be pretty busy for the next couple rotations." Haez grinned down and then turned his attention to his mothers.

"We're finalizing all the paperwork today. You're looking at Riluuk's newest security consulting company."

Boli and Genn seemed to both let out breaths of relief. If there was anything that signaled their intent to stay, it was starting a business together.

"That's wonderful, sweetheart! You really should get that horn sealed before you take on any clients," Boli said, smile grimacing a little as she gave another worried look at the jagged stump. Haez waved her off.

"It looks rugged," he said dismissively.

"It looks unprofessional. And it could split again."

"If you don't mind my asking," Genn started, grabbing a piece of fruit with her hook, "why security consulting? Doesn't seem related to your jobs."

The silence that fell over the room was deafening. Sonia and Haez both squirmed at the question and looked to each other, unsure how to answer. Boli cleared her throat and shot a look to Genn, who quickly swallowed down her food.

"It sounds like a great idea," Genn said in a rush. "If there's anything that me and your mom can do to help, you know you got it."

"Thanks, Ma," Haez said. As Boli started on him again about the horn and infection risks if he left it, Sonia stood from the bench and quietly excused herself. She got a container from the kitchen and filled it with a bit of everything from the breakfast platter—fruit, fluffy balls of sweet bread dotted with seeds, and the slivers of raw meat that she usually avoided. She closed the lid, tied a string around it to keep it shut, and slid it into a light satchel that hung by the door. Slinging the satchel across her body, she exited onto the bark ledge outside.

Even with the advanced medicine that Riluuk doctors had to offer, it had taken the better part of their time on Ghusn for Sonia's ankle to heal. The day prior, she had finally been given the okay to stop wearing a brace. Still, she tested it carefully and made sure to flex and stretch once outside the door. Today, she was determined to get to the forest floor under her own power.

There were lifts that ran up the sides of the trees and connected all levels, and beside them were the ladders. They were little more than a safety formality that hardly saw use even when lifts broke down. But the weeks of inactivity had Sonia's skin itching and she missed the muscle-burn and finger-bite of climbing. Haez had made her promise to not try freeclimbing on her first time out, so she begrudgingly agreed to stick with the ladders.

Within minutes of descending, she felt her anxieties and restlessness melt away with each breath of petrichor that filled her lungs and every brush of wind that cooled the sweat of her brow. Time faded away and she was startled when she went to take another step down only to hit solid ground.

It was quiet on the forest floor—nothing but the rustling of animals brave enough to live at the city's feet and the occasional scattered walker who also needed the meditative calm of soil underfoot. Haez had brought her down on the lifts while she was still healing and helped her walk a short distance from the home tree to find a spot she had liked. She returned there now, the first time coming here alone since arriving.

Pushing through a cluster of bushes, she found the small clearing. In the centre was a little metal plate jammed into the ground in front of a brilliantly coloured flowering plant.

"Morning, Dad," Sonia muttered to the makeshift tombstone. She cleared away what remained of the food she had left the last time she was there, throwing the scraps into the bushes for the animals and laying out a fresh meal in front of the roughly engraved name plate. Haez had helped her choose a toxic local plant to place overtop to discourage any scavenging animals from disturbing the site. Not that there was much other than bone and metal—she didn't have the heart to bury everything, and Ottok's large, central piercing now hung from a chain around Sonia's neck.

"It's the big day today. We should be able to start taking on clients next week. Not that there's much crime to protect against, but we'll make it work." She rambled absently like that for a long time, sitting with her back to a stone and looking up towards the treetops. It was about everything and nothing, just the way she used to talk to him—sitting at the kitchen nook as he navigated the scrap piles.

At least he gets to be somewhere beautiful in the end, she thought.

Distantly, there was the ding and swish of a lift door opening followed by the crunch of footsteps towards the clearing. Haez pushed through the bushes and sat on the stone behind Sonia, wrapping his arms around her.

"How's the old man?" he asked.

"Oh, talking my ear off, as usual."

Haez chuckled and after a moment, he quietly asked, "How do you feel? You sure you're ready to commit to this place?"

"Yeah," she said, taking a breath and squinting up towards the sky and the sunbeams streaming in between the trees. "I feel like I'm home."

Acknowledgements

Welcome to the end and thank you for making it here! Its hard to believe that this little book that started as a fun diversion from screen-writing is now here, in your hands or on your ereader. Handsome Devil wouldn't have been able to happen without my family, friends, and collaborators—this is your book as much as it is mine.

To my partner, who requested to be called "Marf", and my son, who cannot make such requests as he is a toddler—you two are the lights of my life and give me the motivation everyday to be the best possible version of myself. If creativity is a garden, you are the hearty layer of stinky fertilizer that cultivates it. I joke, but one of you does still poop your pants.

To my mother, who took a question about how to throw a self-published book on Amazon and established us a whole ass publishing company. You are insane, feral, and absolutely correct. Thank you for sharing the burden of this overwhelming endeavor so I could produce something worthwhile.

To my father, who has given my little family an unfathomable amount of support while navigating our first year as parents and who taught me that happiness is worth more than money. I'll never be able to thank you enough, Dad. I'm working hard every day to try to be as good a parent to my child as you've been to me.

To Nyco, our incredible cover artist and the best collaborator I could have asked for. The amount of energy and care you've put into telling this story is second only to me—and even that's debatable. Thank you for seeing the vision and helping me realize it. My words may have given Quantrin existence, but your artwork gave it life.

To Gem, my dearest friend, loudest cheerleader, and the most world's most understanding copyeditor. I cannot believe my luck that I have the privilege to be friends with a treasure such as yourself. Thank you for giving me the words I needed at the time when I needed them.

To Lillian, who had the mighty task of doing the first edit. You really knew how to make my story shine and I feel like I'm coming away from this as a better writer due to your insights. Also, I am sorry—I really thought I knew how to use semi-colons.

To Sam, Amy, Michelle, and Carlie—the original fans of Handsome Devil. Thank you for being kind to the quivering and vulnerable mess of the early drafts. Thank you more for being critical enough to train it into being a bad bitch.

To my horrible cats. You know what you did.

Lastly, to the readers who are taking a chance on an unknown author with her weird little book in a genre that she made up a name for. I cannot thank you enough for deciding that Handsome Devil was worth your time and money—goodness knows none of us have enough of either. I hope you had as much fun reading as I had writing.

Sincerely,
Gael Romer

About the author

Gael Romer is a disgracefully obvious Scorpio who spends her time staying dry in her temperate rainforest city and feeding bits of grilled cheese sandwich to the local crows. When she's not writing about handsome aliens, she's recording a Star Wars podcast with her friends and ranting to anyone who will listen about the Baby Ludi lore.

Connect online

gaelromer.com

www.ingramcontent.com/pod-product-compliance
Lightning Source LLC
Chambersburg PA
CBHW031305120726
47906CB00003B/893